It was bound in brown suede leather, sort of fat and floppy, and held together with thick brown cord. Printed on the leather in black marker were the words CHICKEN EMERGENCY.

The pages had a covering of some kind of thin clear plastic, and newspaper clippings were neatly trimmed and pasted to the pages.

The first clipping was a picture of a white-haired guy with a big scissors, cutting a ribbon over a manhole. The caption read MAYOR DEDICATES NEW SEWER.

Next was an article without a picture: CLAM FEVER SCARE OVER! "WAS MERELY OVEREATING," SAYS DOCTOR.

Then there was a picture of a first-grade class at Hoboken Elementary that had made a giant map of New Jersey out of empty cigarette packages.

"Nothing about a chicken emergency," Bruno Ugg said.

"Look at this article!" I said.

Also available by Daniel Pinkwater

DANIEL PINKWATER

LOOKING FOR BOBOWICZ

A HOBOKEN CHICKEN STORY

ILLUSTRATED BY
JILL PINKWATER

HarperTrophy®
An Imprint of HarperCollinsPublishers

Looking for Bobowicz
Text copyright © 2004 by Daniel Pinkwater
Illustrations copyright © 2004 by Jill Pinkwater

Library of Congress Cataloging-in-Publication Data
Pinkwater, Daniel Manus, 1941–
    Looking for Bobowicz : a Hoboken chicken story /
Daniel Pinkwater ; illustrated by Jill Pinkwater.—1st ed.
        p.   cm.
    Summary: Upon moving to Hoboken, New Jersey, a boy
convinces his two new friends to help him track down
the mysterious phantom who stole his bicycle, as well as
Arthur Bobowicz, owner of a giant chicken that once
terrorized local citizens.
    ISBN-10: 0-06-053556-3 — ISBN-13: 978-0-06-053556-8
    [1. Eccentrics and eccentricities—Fiction. 2. City and
town life—Fiction. 3. Moving, Household—Fiction.
4. Hoboken (N. J.)—Fiction. 5. Humorous stories.]
I. Pinkwater, Jill, ill. II. Title.
PZ7.P6335Lo 2004
[Fic]—dc22   2003021440

Typography by Andrea Vandergrift
❖
First Harper Trophy edition, 2006

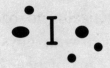

·I·

On Friday I had my last day at Happy Valley Elementary School. On Saturday the moving truck came and took all our stuff to Hoboken, New Jersey, and we left our house in Happy Valley forever. On Sunday, our first day in the new house, the temperature was one hundred degrees Fahrenheit—the beginning of the hottest heat wave ever recorded in Hoboken in the month of June for 120 years.

One hundred and twenty years ago was when our Hoboken house had been built. This is what my parents did. They gave up a modern house in Happy Valley, New Jersey—a house with a front yard, a backyard, and trees, on a street with similar houses and similar trees—to move to a brick house with no front yard, practically no backyard, and no trees, on a street with guys sitting on the steps drinking cans of beer and spitting on the sidewalk, and cars and buses running right past our door. And the Hoboken house was in rotten condition and cost three times as much as we got for our Happy Valley house.

My parents said we were going to fix up the house and have an "urban lifestyle." This is what an urban lifestyle is: My bike was stolen the first hour we were in town. And it was one hundred degrees Fahrenheit. My mother said she didn't want me growing up in a suburb. She said life was real in cities. I went upstairs to sit in my crummy 120-year-old room.

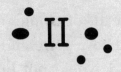

My father climbed the stairs to my room.

"Egad! It's hot as an oven in here, old pal," he said.

My father says things like "egad" and "odds bodkin." They have no meaning. I simply tolerate these weirdnesses, along with so many things my parents do.

"Sorry about your bike, old man," my father said.

He calls me *old man*, also *old chap*. There is no explanation for this.

"We'll get you another bike, I promise," he said. "But could you possibly wait until your birthday? There are a lot of expenses fixing up the new house."

This was great. I could have a bike for my

birthday, instead of some other present, which I would have gotten if I was not to get a bike, which I would not be getting if the one I already had hadn't been stolen, which it probably would not have been if we had not moved to Hoboken, which was not my idea in the first place.

Okay, it wasn't a great bike. My mother had gotten it for me at a garage sale. It was one of those shorty models, for little kids— not the on-purpose low-slung kind with the banana seat and the fake roll bar. Those too are uncool, but this was just like a shrunken normal bike. And it was a girl's bike. It was light blue with pink hearts and flowers painted on the frame. I had removed the white wicker basket with plastic flowers, but it still looked girly. Also the front wheel had a bad wiggle, and the brakes didn't really work. So it was an awful bike—it was still mine—it was transportation—and somebody had stolen it—and it wasn't my idea to move to Hoboken—and it wasn't a very nice thing to happen to me right away on my first day.

"That will be fine, Dad," I said.

"Good show, old man," my father said. "Now about this room ... I don't see how you can stand it. Maybe you'd like us to drag your mattress into our room, where it's nice and cool."

My parents' bedroom had a little dinky air conditioner that puffed air about three degrees cooler than what was outside. It was pathetic.

"I'll be fine here, Dad," I said.

"Good lad. Now do you want to help us scrape paint off the woodwork or just explore around?"

"I think I'll do some exploring," I said.

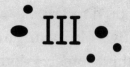

III

I had already had a quick look at the basement, and I wanted to go back. It was huge! It went on forever. It was very deep, which gave it a high ceiling, and it was full of wonderful junk!

The house may have been 120 years old, but at least two hundred years' worth of stuff was piled up in the basement. Things were piled up so that you couldn't make out separate objects all at once. At first it looked like a giant tangle, and then, in the light of the bare lightbulbs, you'd start to see individual things, one at a time.

There was a workbench, covered with dust, and a few rusty tools. There were boxes and cartons and crates and coffee cans full of

6

screws and nails. There was a bumper off a car, about fifteen busted tennis racquets, a stack of old-time TV sets piled one on top of another, a coil of wire that was as thick as my finger, a stuffed swordfish with a busted beak, (that was going on the wall in my room, I decided right away). And then I saw it. The fan!

It was a big fan, four feet in diameter, on a metal stand, like a flagpole. It was much taller than me. I had never seen anything like it. I plugged it into the electrical box behind the workbench and threw the switch. There was a buzzing noise, then a grinding, and the big blades began to turn in their metal cage. The whole top of the thing turned left and right, and as it picked up speed, it blew gritty dust everywhere. It worked! But it needed help. I switched it off. And pulled the plug.

I found a pair of pliers and a screwdriver, also a can of oil and some rags. I was going to have to take the thing apart, clean and oil it, and then get it upstairs to my bedroom. There would be no way to take it up in one piece.

The base on which it stood must have weighed fifty pounds. I would have to sort of roll it up the stairs, resting on every step. The idea was, once I got the pieces up to my bedroom, I would put it together and have a cool room in more ways than one.

It took the rest of the day. I was pretty tired and dirty and oily and sweaty when I got the thing upstairs and back together, but it was worth it. It had cleaned up beautifully, and I had squirted oil into the little oil holes in the motor and along the spindle. When I plugged it in and switched it on, it made a lovely humming noise and turned its huge head from side to side. I found I had to put a pile of books on each corner of my bed to keep the sheets from blowing off. After that it was cool sleeping for me, right through the muggy, mosquito-infested, Hoboken heat-wave night.

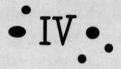

IV

In the morning the sun came up looking like a red-hot penny. You could tell it was going to be another scorching day, the kind where you can fry an egg on the sidewalk. I stepped out the front door, intending to maybe do some exploring, and the heat smacked me in the face. I stepped back into the house. My parents were getting ready to go to work in air-conditioned offices in New York City, across the river. I was on my own.

I thought it might be a good idea to rummage around in the basement some more. The fan had been a good find, and it looked as though there was a lot more interesting stuff piled up in the dark corners. Also it would be cool down there—anyway, cooler.

There were two naked lightbulbs that hung down on their wires. You turned them on by pulling a string. Until you got to the first lightbulb, you had to make your way by the light that shone down the basement steps. It was a little scary and a little dangerous.

As I got to the bottom of the steps, and before I pulled the string on the first light, I thought I saw a dim blue-green glow coming from way back where it was darkest.

I stood and looked, opening my eyes as wide as I could. What could be making that light? When I turned the light on, I couldn't see it, and when I turned it off again, there it was. I tried to memorize the location and moved toward it, turning the lights on as I went.

I had to climb over some stuff—rusty bedsprings, broken furniture, things like that. Then I found the source of the greenish glow. There was a brick removed from the wall, up near the ceiling and way back in the basement. I stood on a little wooden barrel and was able to see that the brick behind had been removed, and the brick behind that, all the way through the wall and into the basement of the building next door. Obviously a pipe or something had once run between the buildings.

There was a light on in the other basement, and I could hear muffled voices and music. I don't know why I did this, but I put my mouth to the hole and hooted like an owl. "Whooo! Whooo!" The voices stopped.

"Whooo! Whooo!" The music stopped.

I thought I heard whispering.

Then I heard a voice come through the hole. "Is there somebody there?"

"I am Edmund Dantes," I said. "I have been unjustly imprisoned by my enemies." I got this from a Classics Comic of my father's—he saved them from his childhood and he lets me read them. This one was *The Count of Monte Cristo*. I'd like to read the actual book someday.

"I am the Abbe Faria," the voice said. "A priest, also unjustly imprisoned in the Chateau d'If."

That was incredible! The Abbe Faria is another character in the story. "How'd you know what I was talking about?" I asked into the hole.

"We've got about a hundred Classics Comics down here," the voice said. "You want to come over?"

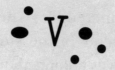

V

I went next door. It was just like our house, only it was divided into apartments. It wasn't hard to find the door that led to the basement. There I found a boy and a girl, about my age. The boy would have been beautiful, if he were a girl. The girl would have been handsome, if she were a boy.

"Why is your hair like that?" the girl asked me.

"I sleep in front of a powerful fan," I said.

"My name is Loretta Fischetti," the girl said. "This is my friend Bruno Ugg. Bruno will not speak to you. He is not being rude. He took a vow of silence and can't speak to anyone. Bruno, when did you take the vow of silence?"

"Six o'clock yesterday. Rats! I talked! Now I have to start all over again!" Bruno Ugg said.

"You see how it is," Loretta Fischetti said. "What's your name?"

"Call me Nick," I said.

"Nick? That's your name?"

"Not my real name."

"No?"

"No. It's my nickname."

"I see. Your nickname is Nick."

"That's right."

"What's your real name?"

"Do you have to know?"

"Yes. We have to know."

"My real name is Ivan."

"Ivan what?"

"Ivan Itch."

"Your name is Itch? Ivan Itch? Are you telling the truth?"

"Yes. It was a longer name that ended in *itch*, and my great-grandfather shortened it."

"Because he thought it sounded funny?"

"Yes."

"So he shortened it to *Itch*?"

"I think he was dyslexic."

"And then your parents named you Ivan?"

"Ivan was my great-grandfather's name."

"What do you think of this guy?" Loretta Fischetti asked Bruno Ugg.

"He can hang out with us. Oh, dang! I talked!" Bruno Ugg looked at his watch and made a note on a little piece of paper. He was recording the time he had begun his vow of silence—again.

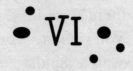

VI

"**S**o what are you guys doing down here?" I asked.

"Are you kidding? It's another scorcher out there. People are frying eggs," Loretta Fischetti said. "We're keeping cool underground. So you read *The Count of Monte Cristo*?"

"Just the Classics Comic," I said.

"That's what I meant," Loretta Fischetti said.

"Alexandre Dumas wrote the story—I forget who drew the pictures," I said. "I—that is, my father—has *The Three Musketeers* and *The Man in the Iron Mask*, also by him."

"Could we read them?" Bruno Ugg asked. "Oh, stinkfish! I talked again!" He made another note on his little piece of paper.

"I'll go get them," I said.

"Bring all you've got," Loretta Fischetti said. "We can swap around."

"Not for keeps," I said. "They're really my dad's."

The whole time we were talking, there was this amazing music playing on an old radio Loretta and Bruno had in the basement. It was music I knew I had never heard before, and yet it all sounded familiar, one song after another. It was a little difficult paying attention to what we were saying because of the music, and in fact we had been speaking slower than we might have normally.

"What is this music?" I asked Loretta Fischetti.

"That's Radio Jolly Roger," she said. "It's a pirate radio station. The guy who runs it plays only songs from the past . . . old blues, cowboy songs, hillbilly music, stuff like that. It's cool, isn't it?"

Just then we heard a voice over the radio: "That was 'Crab Apple Blues' by Memphis

Melvin, and this is WRJR, Radio Jolly Roger, in beautiful Hoboken, where the sewer meets the sea, bringing you the finest in recorded music."

"That's Vic Trola," Loretta Fischetti said. "He's my favorite disc jockey on WRJR."

"He's the only disc jockey on WRJR," Bruno Ugg said.

"No he's not," Loretta Fischetti said. "There's Boppin' Bob, and Doctor Secundra Dass, the classical music guy."

"They're all the same person! They're all him! And I spoke again and ruined my vow of silence, blast it!" Bruno Ugg said.

"That's Bruno's theory," Loretta Fischetti said. "He might be right. Anyway, Vic Trola is my favorite."

"He's got a multiple personality. Oops! Doggone it!" Bruno Ugg said, and once more scratched out the starting time on the little piece of paper and wrote in a new one.

"I'll go get my dad's Classics Comics," I said.

"It would be a nice gesture if you brought

bottles of Dr. Pedwee's Grape Soda, available at the corner store, on the way back," Loretta Fischetti said. "I think I have some money somewhere."

"It will be my treat," I said.

"I'd like Dr. Pedwee's Raspberry," Bruno Ugg said. Then he said, "Oh, heck!"

"Why did you want to take a vow of silence, anyway?" I asked Bruno Ugg.

"Just to see if I could do it. . . . Dagnabbit! I spoke again!"

"I'll be back in a few," I said.

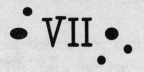

VII

The radio in the little corner store was playing a cowboy song. I guessed it was that same radio station. Then I heard Vic Trola announce, "That was 'Blood on the Saddle,' sung by Tex Ritter." It was Radio Jolly Roger, all right.

There was a counter with five stools, a display case full of candy bars, a wall rack with newspapers in English, Italian, Spanish, German, and some other languages that use different alphabets, Arabic maybe, or Hebrew, or Russian. I recognized Chinese. There was a fan, like the one in my bedroom, turning left and right, blowing the hot air around. On shelves there was everything from soap powder and dog food to spark plugs and panty hose.

There was a redheaded guy behind the counter. He stuck out his hand.

"Welcome to my little shop, fine young gentleman. I am Sean Vergessen."

I shook his hand. "Call me Nick," I said.

"That your real name?" Sean Vergessen asked.

"Why wouldn't it be?" I asked.

"I don't know," Sean Vergessen said. "I just thought it might be a . . . nickname." He giggled.

"I want a bottle of Dr. Pedwee's Grape Soda, a bottle of Dr. Pedwee's Raspberry, and a bottle of . . . "

"May I suggest Dr. Pedwee's Grapefruit-Lime," Sean Vergessen said. "It's refreshing and delightful. By the way, you've never been in here before, have you?"

"We just moved in," I said.

"Oh! You're the kid who had his bike stolen!" Sean Vergessen said.

"How did you know that?" I asked, surprised.

"I hear things," Sean Vergessen said.

"Do you know who took it?" I asked.

"Tell you what, young Nick," Sean Vergessen said. "Since you are new to the neighborhood and this is your first time in my store, the sodas are on the house, and here's a bag of fried pork rinds, also free." He put the bottles and the bag of pork rinds into my backpack, into which I had already put my father's collection of Classics Comics.

"So do you know who took my bike?" I asked.

"Well, I have to go in the back and . . . count things," Sean Vergessen said. "I'm sure you have many things to do also."

The next thing I knew, I was outside in the street.

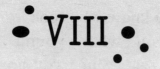

VIII

The basement in Loretta Fischetti's and Bruno Ugg's building wasn't dark and full of stuff like mine. There was linoleum on the floor and hideous blue-green paint on the walls. There were a couple of beat-up sofas and a big easy chair, also crummy. There was a washing machine and a dryer, and of course the old radio. Light came from fluorescent tubes on the ceiling. Bruno and Loretta had their Classics Comics in a plastic milk crate.

"I'm back," I said. "I have sodas."

"Gimme," Bruno Ugg said.

"Give up on the vow of silence?" I asked.

"It wasn't working out," Bruno said. "Loretta kept tricking me into talking."

"I'm twice as smart as he is," Loretta said.

"Tricking him is pathetically easy."

"That being the case," Bruno said, "I don't see what pleasure it gives you to mess with my head."

"It's my way of showing affection," Loretta said. "Are the pork rinds for us?"

"Help yourselves," I said. "Sean Vergessen gave me the whole works for free, because I'm new."

"Nice gesture," Bruno Ugg said.

"Say, what's the deal with Sean Vergessen?" I asked.

"What do you mean?" Loretta Fischetti asked back.

"Is he all right, or what?"

"Well, for an adult, I'd say he's pretty all right."

"How come he didn't want to talk about who stole my bike?" I asked.

"Ohhh, you're the one whose bike was stolen!"

"Yes, and Vergessen seemed to know all about it, but he wouldn't say who took it."

"That's because he's D and D," Loretta Fischetti said.

"D and D?" I asked.

"Deaf and Dumb," Loretta Fischetti said. "Old tradition on the waterfront. It's considered bad manners to name names."

"We sort of knew about it too," Bruno Ugg said. "Of course, we didn't know it was your bike exactly."

"Do you know who took it?" I asked. "I'd really like to get it back."

"It's not so much a who as a what," Loretta said.

"A what?"

"Yes. There's a sort of . . . phantom that hangs around."

"A phantom? What do you mean?"

"You know, a mysterious figure, possibly human, possibly something else, lurks in the shadows, menaces people, does things."

"Does things?"

"Like your bike."

"So you think a phantom took it?"

"It's just an educated guess."

"Why not just some normal thief?"

"Well, from what I heard, it's a really crappy bike. What normal thief would want it?"

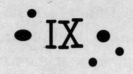

IX

All this time Jolly Roger Radio was playing in the background—guys twanging guitars or blowing on jugs, songs about faithless love, having the blues, herding cattle, and shooting people with a pistol as long as your arm. Bruno Ugg had pulled my father's stack of Classics Comics out of my backpack and was dividing them into two piles—ones they had read already and ones they hadn't.

"It doesn't only do bad things," he said.

"The phantom?"

"Sometimes it leaves little presents," Loretta Fischetti said.

"You'll wake up in the morning, and there on the foot of your bed will be a piece of broken machinery, or a brick, or maybe half a tuna fish sandwich," Bruno Ugg said.

"Has anything like that happened to you personally?" I asked.

"Maybe," Bruno Ugg said.

"D and D," Loretta Fischetti said.

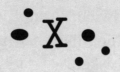

X

"I have dibs on *The Three Musketeers*!" Bruno Ugg said.

"Okay, I'll read *The Man in the Iron Mask*, and then we'll swap," Loretta Fischetti said.

"I'd wait and read *The Three Musketeers* first," I said. "*The Man in the Iron Mask* is sort of a sequel."

"Thanks," Loretta Fischetti said. "Let's see what Jules Verne ones you've got."

"*Around the World in Eighty Days.*"

"Already read it."

"Did you read *Twenty Thousand Leagues Under the Sea*?"

"No! Is that by him? I've heard of it."

Loretta Fischetti grabbed my copy of

Twenty Thousand Leagues Under the Sea and her bottle of Dr. Pedwee's Grape and flopped into the broken-down armchair.

I flipped through the Classics Comics in the milk crate, selected *The Hunchback of Notre Dame* by Victor Hugo, and got comfortable on the sofa that wasn't occupied by Bruno Ugg.

The morning passed like that. While the sidewalks got egg-frying hot, we sprawled in the cool basement, listening to the sweet sounds of Radio Jolly Roger, sipping the sweet sodas, crunching the pork rinds, and turning pages.

After *The Hunchback of Notre Dame*, which was good, I read *Dr. Jekyll and Mr. Hyde*, which was better. Bruno handed over *The Three Musketeer*s to Loretta when he was finished, and then read *The Man in the Iron Mask*.

At one point Mrs. Fischetti, Loretta's mother, came down to do laundry. At lunchtime Bruno Ugg's mother brought us bologna sandwiches and glasses of milk.

By midafternoon, about the time I started reading *Oliver Twist*, Loretta Fischetti and Bruno Ugg were my best friends.

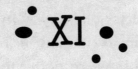

XI

"**W**hat did you do all day, old bean?" my father asked.

"I met a couple of kids on the block."

"Nice blokes?"

"One bloke and one . . . blokette," I said. "And they seem pretty nice. They have even more Classics Comics than you. We've been sort of swapping around, but not for keeps. It's all right, isn't it?"

"Do they have *The Corsican Brothers* by Alexandre Dumas?" my father asked.

"I don't know," I said.

"If they have it, ask if I may borrow it," my father said. "It's a cracking good yarn."

"Dad, are you English?"

"Why no, old thing. I was born in Jersey

City, as you very well know. Why do you ask?"

"No reason. Is it okay if I go with my friends tonight? We're going to try to catch bats."

"Bats are tricky little blighters. See that you don't get rabies and die," my father said.

"Actually, I don't think there's much chance of getting near one. Bruno Ugg—one of my new friends—seems to think you can catch a bat by throwing your hat at it."

"It seems unlikely," my father said. "All the same, if you should get bitten, tell me at once so I can arrange for the series of painful shots."

"Thanks, Dad," I said.

"Have fun, Ivan," my father said.

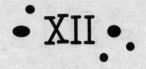

XII

Alexandre Dumas was born in 1802. He was the son of a general in Napoleon's army. His grandmother was a black Haitian slave, and he was proud of her. He was fat, wrote 650 books, had all kinds of adventures, fought in revolutions, hunted big game, had a big yacht, traveled all over, was very rich and spent it all, and was the most famous writer in France and the most famous Frenchman in the world. He died in 1870 and is my father's favorite Classics Comics author. All but that last bit I learned from reading in the back of the Classics Comic of *The Three Musketeers*. I think my father has also read some of Alexandre Dumas's books in the full-length version. I know I am going to tackle *The Man in the Iron Mask* someday.

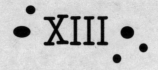

XIII

My mother was sitting on the floor in the middle of the living room with a rag wrapped around her head. She was taking a break from prying up five layers of crummy linoleum to expose the original crummy wooden flooring.

"Going out?" she asked me.

"Going to catch bats with my new friends," I said.

"See? We just arrived, and already you're doing urban things. You're interacting with urban children. Didn't I tell you moving to Hoboken would be good for you?"

Here's what I was thinking: I am supposedly going to hurl my baseball cap at flying rats who might be rabid, and the fact that I have almost no hope of catching one makes it only slightly less an insane thing to do. Also, while Loretta Fischetti and Bruno Ugg are obviously really nice kids, my mother doesn't know that—we could all be setting out to rob a bank. Finally, the fact that I have agreed to go out at night and play bat-hat should be proof to my mother that I have no will of my own and could be influenced to do any kind of foolish or dangerous thing.

Here's what I said to my mother: "Yes, Mom, you sure were right. Urban life is really interesting."

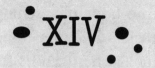

XIV

I met Loretta Fischetti and Bruno Ugg in the street. Loretta Fischetti had a beret, and Bruno Ugg had a regular felt snap-brim hat, like people used to wear—you see them in movies. I was wearing my Happy Valley Walruses baseball hat.

The walrus was the mascot of Happy Valley High School, where I'd expected all my life to go. There was an old belief that the early inhabitants would put out to sea by way of the seventy-three-mile-long Shwamapo River and hunt walruses. My father said it was highly unlikely that there were many walruses off the coast of New Jersey, and the early inhabitants were probably smuggling goods off ships without paying the import tax. Just the same, all the Happy Valley High School teams were called the Fighting Walruses, and our grade-school teams were called the Junior Walruses.

"I see you've got your hat," Loretta Fischetti said. "Let's be on our way to the park—it will be dark soon."

As we walked through the streets of Hoboken on the way to the park, I noticed numerous other kids going in the same direction. Loretta Fischetti and Bruno Ugg appeared to know some of the kids and waved or said hello to them. They introduced me to a few. All the other kids were wearing hats.

When we got to the park, I saw at least one hundred kids—probably closer to two hundred. Every one of them was wearing a hat. I saw cowboy hats, derbies, Mexican sombreros, hunting caps with earflaps, beanies, straw farmer hats, fancy ladies' hats with flowers, sailor hats, top hats like the ones magicians pull rabbits out of, cop hats, locomotive engineer hats, slouch hats, fedoras, trilbies, homburgs, Tyroleans, boaters, caps, pith helmets, conical wizard hats, knit ski caps, and paper hats.

"It's the Hoboken Bat Hat Festival," Bruno Ugg said.

The kids were checking out the hats, as I was. They were milling all around the park, and more kids, wearing hats, were arriving every minute.

"What goes on?" I asked.

"As I said, it's the Hoboken Bat Hat Festival," Bruno Ugg said. "On a certain night in the summer, kids show up at this park. Real little kids aren't allowed, and older kids, like high schoolers, don't come either—just us middle kids. One day the word goes around town that tonight is the Bat Hat Festival, and we all come here, wearing hats. It's an ancient tradition that goes back to our walrus fisherman ancestors."

"Walruses are mammals," I said.

"You going to argue with ancient tradition?" Bruno Ugg asked me. "The guys who caught them were called walrus fishermen.

I don't make the rules."

"So what happens now?" I asked.

"You will notice that there are street lamps along the paths here in the park," Loretta Fischetti said. "When it gets good and dark, insects are attracted to the street lamps and swarm all around them. And you know what that brings."

"Bats?" I asked.

"Bats. Of course we can't see the bats, because they fly in the darkness above the street lamps, feeding on the insects. When you look at a light, the darkness just beyond it is even darker—and the bats are dark themselves, and fast. So what we do—"

"What we do is," Bruno Ugg said, "we toss our hats up into the darkness, trying to get them above and beyond the street lamps. You toss your hat, and into it flies Mr. Bat. Naturally, once he's in the hat, he can't flap his little leather wings, and the whole thing, bat and hat, comes down to the ground. You pounce on your hat, and bang! you've caught yourself a bat!"

"And then what do you do?" I asked. "What do you do once you've caught the bat?"

Bruno Ugg and Loretta Fischetti looked at each other. Some other kids had gathered around us during the explanation. "What do we do when we catch a bat?" Bruno asked.

"I don't rightly know," Loretta Fischetti said. "No one has ever caught one when I've been here. It's not easy."

"I think someone caught a bat three years ago," Bruno Ugg said.

· XV ·

The streetlights had come on, and the purple twilight was turning to blackness. Fireflies blinked in the branches of the trees. The kids spread out along the paths in Tesev Noskecnil Park, named after some hero of the past—probably one of those walrus fishermen, I thought.

Loretta Fischetti, Bruno Ugg, and I staked out a length of path near a streetlight and waited. The others took their hats off, so I did too.

It was getting darker by the second. I could hear kids shouting in different parts of the park.

"The bats are here! The bats are here!"

"I think I saw one! I think I saw one!"

"Hush! Quiet! You have to listen for the squeaking!"

"Shlermie! Where's Shlermie?"

Kids were starting to run back and forth and toss their hats.

"Whoo! Good one!"

"See how high mine went?"

"Shlermie, where are you?"

"I think I got one! I think I got one! I got one! I got one! Awww, rats! I didn't get one!"

"Look! Look! There's a bat! Throw your hat!"

"Hey! My hat is stuck in a tree!"

"Shlermie! Are you here?"

"Will you look out? Quit bumping into me!"

"Euwww! I stepped in something!"

"There's more bats over here!"

"You're standing on my hat!"

"I can't see the bats! Where are they?"

"Here, bats! Nice bats! Come here, bats!"

"Idiot! Bats won't come when you call them!"

"A bat just flew over my head! Really! I swear!"

"Ow! I ran into a tree!"

"Shlermeeee!"

At first I was tossing my hat in the air like all the others. Then, as I ran back and forth and listened to all the shouting, I began to shout too, and then I began to laugh. I noticed that Loretta Fischetti and Bruno Ugg were laughing. Everybody was laughing. After a while I was laughing so hard I couldn't do anything else. I got out of breath and bent over with my hands on my knees, laughing. Then I sank to the ground and just lay there laughing so hard my eyes filled with tears. My stomach muscles hurt from laughing so hard. Just about everyone else was on the ground too, rolling back and forth and waving arms and legs and laughing until all we could do was sort of sob and giggle.

Bruno Ugg was lying near me, flat on his back. He was the first to get control of himself. I heard him say, "The good old Bat Hat Festival. Always a success."

I sat up and was feeling around for my hat when I noticed, at the very edge of the park, barely catching the light from one of the street lamps, a tall figure, very tall, dressed in a long black coat—more of a cape—with a hood. As I watched, the tall figure in black mounted a small girl's bike, light blue, with pink hearts and flowers painted on the frame.

"Look! That . . . that . . . phantom's got my bike!" I said, just as it rode away into the darkness.

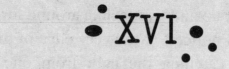

XVI

All over Tesev Noskecnil Park, kids were pulling themselves together, dusting themselves off, and looking for their hats. They walked out of the park and headed for home down various streets, in twos and threes and little bunches.

"Wow! So you actually saw the phantom!" Bruno Ugg said.

"Well, I saw something that looked to me like a phantom," I said. "And it had my bike."

"You lucky pup," Loretta Fischetti said. "Hardly anyone has ever seen the phantom. People just have things stolen or wake up to find a broken toaster oven in their room."

"Or they hear strange noises in the night," Bruno Ugg said. "Excuse me for changing the subject, but do you know who used to live in this house?"

We had just left the park and were at the top of River Street. There was an ordinary brick house, the kind that has three or four apartments. There was an iron fence in front and a little garden.

"No idea," I said. "Was it a walrus fisherman?"

"This house, once upon a time, was the residence of Gugliermo Marconi," Bruno Ugg said proudly.

"And who was that? A rock star?" I asked.

"You mean to stand there and tell us you don't know who Gugliermo Marconi was?" Loretta Fischetti asked.

"Not only do I not know who he was, I have no hope of pronouncing his name," I said. "So who was he already?"

"Did you ever hear of a thing called radio?" Bruno Ugg asked.

"Of course I have heard of a thing called radio," I said. "I suppose you are going to tell me that this Marconi guy invented it."

"Bingo!" Loretta Fischetti said.

"What?" I asked. "No kidding?"

"No kidding."

"That's a pretty big invention," I said. "And he lived here?"

"So we are told," Bruno Ugg said.

The apartment on the first floor had a picture window, and we could see right into the living room. It wasn't a normal living room. It was part living room and part something else. A guy in a white shirt, wearing earphones on his head, was sitting at a sort of table with lights and switches and a big microphone in front of him.

"That wouldn't be the guy himself, would it?" I asked. "He looks kind of goofy to be a famous inventor."

The guy in the earphones was motioning for us to come inside.

"He's no Marconi," Loretta Fischetti said. "This guy is Vic Trola."

We crowded into the apartment. When Vic Trola talked, I recognized his voice immediately.

"Kids, I'm dying for a Dr. Pedwee's Double

Fudge. If you'll run over to Washington Street and get me a couple, there's a buck plus three sodas in it for you."

Five minutes later we were back in Vic Trola's combination living room and disk jockey studio with cold bottles of Dr. Pedwee's soda, sitting on the old sofa and watching him do his radio show.

There were cardboard egg cartons stapled all over the walls and ceiling, and it felt like four or five thicknesses of carpet under our feet. That was to absorb noise, Vic Trola explained to us.

Vic Trola held a finger to his lips, signaling us to be quiet. "That was 'Chicken on a Raft Blues' by Blind Fig," he said into the microphone while slipping an old-fashioned non-stereo phonograph record into its brown paper sleeve, sliding out another one, putting it on a turntable, and lowering the tone arm onto the rim.

"Now we'll hear Cowboy Steve and his Chuck Wagon Warblers doing a tune called 'The Old Drooling Drover,'" Vic Trola said while turning the volume up on the turntable, turning the volume down on his microphone, taking a swig of his Dr. Pedwee's, noting the time on his big wall clock, and writing down what record he had just played in his big logbook.

"I have to record everything in the log. Federal regulations," Vic Trola said.

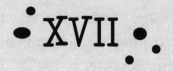

XVII

Vic Trola pointed to us. "You may talk now," he said. "But when I do this"—he made a throat-cutting motion with his hand—"that means, stop talking at once, okay?"

We nodded silently.

"No, it's okay to talk now," Vic Trola said. "I was just demonstrating. But when I do that again, it's dummy-up time, got it?"

"Mr. Trola," Loretta Fischetti began.

"Call me Vic."

"Vic, we thank you for the sodas and the dollar tip," Loretta Fischetti said. "But why couldn't you go over to Washington Street yourself? It's only a short block."

"Regulations," Vic Trola said. "Federal regulations. I can't leave the radio station unattended when it's broadcasting—in case of a natural disaster, or a shipwreck, or something like that."

"But isn't this a pirate radio station?" Loretta Fischetti asked.

"It sure is," Vic Trola said. "See my flag?"

Tacked to the wall was a black pirate flag with skull and crossed bones and the letters *WRJR*.

"I thought a pirate radio station was unlicensed and illegal," Loretta Fischetti said.

"That is so," Vic Trola said.

"In that case, why do you bother about regulations?"

Vic Trola stood up—actually he crouched, since the cord attaching his headset to the desk wasn't long enough to allow him to stand. "Miss, I may be a pirate, but I am also a gentleman."

"Did Marconi, the inventor of radio, actually live in this house?" I asked.

"Some say that wireless radio was invented by J. C. Bose and Marconi falsely patented it and accepted the Nobel Prize for the other guy's invention. Others say that radio was invented by pixies, but I say . . ." The record on the turntable was coming to the end. Vic Trola made the throat-cutting gesture, turned down the volume on the turntable, turned up the volume on the microphone, and said, "These are the sounds of Radio Jolly Roger, in beautiful Hoboken, where the fish are jumping and the cotton is high. We heard 'Blockhead Breakdown' by the Hogboro Jug Band, followed by 'Little Joe the Wrangler,' sung by William Shatner, after which we heard 'Frozen Yogurt Blues' by Blind Persimmon, and lastly 'Goin' Down Disabled Creek' by the Banjo Buccaneers. Stay tuned to Hoboken's own Radio Jolly Roger, WRJR. We play the songs you long for."

Vic Trola pointed to us again.

"You may talk now," he said.

"You were telling us about Marconi, who may have invented radio and whose house this may once have been," I said.

"Did you know the first organized baseball game was played in Hoboken, in eighteen forty-six?" Vic Trola asked. "And the first steam-driven railroad locomotive in America was built here in eighteen twenty-five. Stephen Foster, the most famous songwriter of the nineteenth century, lived here—so did a lot of writers and artists. It has the oldest engineering college, the famous Clam Broth House restaurant, and Frank Sinatra, a big singer, was born here."

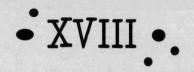

XVIII

"You know a lot about Hoboken," Bruno Ugg said.

"It's my hobby," Vic Trola said.

"Do you know anything about the phantom?" I asked.

"What?"

"The phantom. Do you know anything about it?"

"Sorry, kids. You have to go," Vic Trola said.

"We have to go? We haven't finished our Dr. Pedwee's!"

"Take them with you. Sorry. You can't hang around the radio station. Federal regulations." Vic Trola was waving his arms at us, shooing us out the door.

The next thing we knew we were outside in the street.

"Bye-bye, kids!" Vic Trola shouted as he pulled the curtains across the picture window. "Keep listening to Radio Jolly Roger!"

"That was a little weird," I said.

"Yes, he was perfectly talkative and friendly until we mentioned the phantom," Loretta Fischetti said.

"Then he couldn't get rid of us fast enough," Bruno Ugg said.

"He went D and D," Loretta Fischetti said.

"Yes, Deaf and Dumb," I said.

XIX

C - that's the way you begin.
H - is the next letter in.
I - I am the third.
C - Is the middle of the word.
K - I'm fillin' in.
E - I'm near the end.
C-h-i-c-k-e-n,
That's the way you spell chicken.

That was the song we heard on Radio Jolly Roger. It was hot again, so we had gone underground to listen to music and read Classics Comics in the basement of the building where Loretta Fischetti and Bruno Ugg lived.

"*C-h-i-c-k-e-n*, that's the way you spell chicken." They had to be the dumbest words to any song, ever. But the tune was so good, and the guy who sang the song was so good, that it kept going through my mind. Apparently Vic Trola liked it too, because he played it every fifteen or twenty minutes.

"That song is starting to drive me crazy," Loretta Fischetti said.

"I - I am de thoid," Bruno Ugg sang, imitating the guy on the record. "C - in de middle of de woid."

I was reading *Murders in the Rue Morgue* by Edgar Allan Poe. This is an outstanding Classics Comic in which a French detective named C. Auguste Dupin matches wits with a monster murderer who does horrible crimes in Paris, France. Dupin figures out that the killer is not a human being at all, but an evil ape. He tracks it down in the end. I suspect the comic version does not do the story justice, although it does show lots of blood and scary things.

Bruno Ugg was reading *Moby Dick* by Herman Melville, which I had read previously—it's the story of a loony sea captain

and a white whale. It is one of the top stories on my Nick's Picks list, and I recommend it highly. One of the characters is a
cannibal.

Loretta Fischetti was reading *Don
Quixote* by Miguel de Cervantes, a classic of
Spanish literature, and also about a loony old
man.

And of course Vic Trola was with us by
radio, playing the chicken song in between
the old rock 'n' roll, hillbilly songs, and
blues.

When I told my mother that I was lunch-
ing courtesy of either Bruno Ugg's mother or
Loretta Fischetti's mother, she said that she
ought to at least provide dessert and gave me
some money for the purpose. Only we
decided to have dessert first—in today's case
it was Dreamsicles. Dreamsicles, for those
unfortunate enough not to know, are like
Popsicles, only the outside is orange sherbet
and the middle is vanilla ice cream. They are
very nice on a hot morning, while enjoying
music and literature.

"This is all very nice," Loretta Fischetti said. "But I am getting a little fed up with just lying down here like reptiles. We ought to do something."

XX

"**D**o what? It's not even ten A.M., and people are being roasted alive," Bruno Ugg said.

"Just the same, I feel like getting out of here," Loretta Fischetti said.

"Are you nuts? You'll be a french fry," Bruno Ugg said.

"I don't know," Loretta Fischetti said. "Nick could invite us over to see his basement."

"I have an idea," I said. "Why don't we all go over to my basement?"

"Yes? What's over there that's so good?" Loretta Fischetti asked me.

"Just a lot of old junk," I said. "But you were the one who suggested we go over there."

"No, I suggested you invite us," Loretta Fischetti said. "What sort of old junk?"

"All kinds. Lots of it," I said.

"Books, comics, periodicals?" Bruno Ugg asked.

"I don't know," I said. "Probably. There's everything else there. That's where I found the giant fan."

"The one that gives you the radical hairdo," Loretta Fischetti said.

Loretta had decided that the windblown look was cool.

"That's right. There's a lot of busted and rusted machinery, old furniture, tools, boxes of assorted stuff."

"Let's go there," Bruno Ugg said.

"Yes, let's," I said.

"Nothing is stopping us," Loretta Fischetti said.

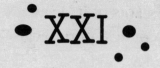

XXI

I had scrounged around my basement a bit, but I had hardly made a dent. There were dark corners and stuff underneath stuff. With my friends, Loretta Fischetti and Bruno Ugg, who had brought along a couple of flashlights, a whole world of junk and treasure turned up.

Here are a few of the things we found:

The stuffed swordfish I mentioned before.

Also a stuffed barracuda.

A lot of busted furniture.

An old-time radio in a wooden cabinet—a floor model, about half the size of a refrigerator. We plugged it in, and after warming up for a while, it played! We tuned in Radio Jolly Roger—Vic Trola was playing the how-to-spell-*chicken* song, of course. The radio sounded great and had a neat red light in the dial.

A canoe! A real canoe! It had a big hole in it, but Bruno Ugg thought we might be able to fix it with a piece of tin from a flattened-out big tomato can and some duct tape.

Four wheels, and all four fenders, plus a door from a small foreign car. There was enough debris piled up that there was a chance we'd find the rest of the car if we kept looking.

Six very old-looking vacuum cleaners.

A bathtub.

An iron potbelly stove.

A cool statue of a tall skinny bird around five feet high and covered with gold—or gold paint.

Fencing foils and masks. We put these aside to clean up and play with later. *The Three Musketeers* was pretty much our group favorite Classics Comic, and these were the best things we had found so far.

Then there were boxes. We found a box completely full of used lightbulbs. Some of them rattled when we shook them and some didn't. We found a box full of white coffee mugs—must have been at least sixty of them. We found a box of old clothes, a box of empty bottles, and a box of cracked and mismatched dishes and bowls.

And then, pay dirt! The mother lode! A box of old comics and magazines. It was too dark to really study what was in it. We dragged it under one of the lights and could see titles like Action Comics, Detective Comics, also old *Life* magazines and paperback books.

"Let's take this back to our basement, which isn't so creepy and dirty, and examine everything," Loretta Fischetti said.

Bruno Ugg and I found some rope, tied it around the box so we'd have something to grab, and together we dragged and lifted it up the stairs, out into the street, and then into Bruno's and Loretta's basement.

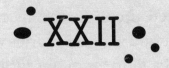

XXII

The *Life* magazines were from the 1950s and 1960s. We didn't know how old the comics were—pretty old, we guessed, maybe from the 1940s, some of them. There was a calendar from 1984 and a newspaper from 1991.

Some of the paperback books—mostly science fiction—had dates in the 1950s printed on that page in the front with all the information. It was mostly pretty old stuff.

"I bet these are worth something," Bruno Ugg said.

"What, old comic books and paperbacks? I doubt it," I said. "But they're interesting."

The comics weren't Classics Comics, but

they looked promising. Some of them had Superman and Batman stories. We decided we would add them to our little collection.

Then we found the scrapbook.

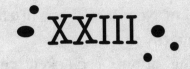

XXIII

It was bound in brown suede leather, sort of fat and floppy, and held together with thick brown cord. Printed on the leather in black marker were the words CHICKEN EMERGENCY.

The pages had a covering of some kind of thin clear plastic, and newspaper clippings were neatly trimmed and pasted to the pages.

The first clipping was a picture of a white-haired guy with a big scissors, cutting a ribbon over a manhole. The caption read MAYOR DEDICATES NEW SEWER.

Next was an article without a picture: CLAM FEVER SCARE OVER! "WAS MERELY OVEREATING," SAYS DOCTOR.

Then there was a picture of a first-grade class at Hoboken Elementary that had made a

giant map of New Jersey out of empty cigarette packages.

"Nothing about a chicken emergency,"
Bruno Ugg said.

"Look at this article!" I said.

·XXIV·

TERROR ON GARDEN STREET

Huge White Creature Sighted by Many

Residents of Garden Street report seeing a very large white animal last night. The animal, which some witnesses identified as a polar bear, was seen running down the street. Other Hoboken residents claim the animal was a white gorilla, because of its ability to climb trees.

Hoboken dog warden Augie Manicotti, asked for comment, said, "All I know is it's not a dog, so it's not my problem."

In addition to a dog warden, Hoboken

has a pussycat warden (an unpaid position) and a rat control officer. These individuals also claimed that their duties did not extend to dealing with animals estimated to be over six feet and well over 200 pounds.

Local zoos and circuses were contacted. None reported losing either a polar bear or a white gorilla.

"Interesting," Loretta Fischetti said.
"Turn the page," Bruno Ugg said.

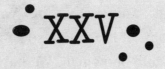

HUGE WHITE ANIMAL TERROR CONTINUES

More Sightings Throughout the City

Many citizens report having seen the very large white creature, first thought to be a polar bear or a white gorilla, but there are many opinions concerning just what kind of animal it is.

"It is a tall, fat man in a white fur coat," Mrs. Gloria Gluckstern, proprietress of Lucky Stars Hairdressers and Pizzeria of River Street, said. "My uncle had a coat like that—and he used to run through the streets too."

Kevin Mookerjee of Washington Street said, "It is a yeti, also known as the Abominable Snowman. We have them in the Himalayas. I often saw them when I was a boy in India."

"It's a big friendly dog," said editor Ed Weiss of Fourteenth Street. "I gave it a doughnut."

Hoboken health commissioner Dr. Milton Sargon of Washington Street believes the white apparition does not exist at all. "Mass hysteria," Dr. Sargon said. "Possibly brought on by the consumption of bad clam juice. People expect to see it, so they see it."

When questioned, Dr. Sargon admitted he had seen it himself.

Hoboken mayor Lawrence Vasolini spoke to the press in his office: "The animal, or fat man in a white fur coat, or group hallucination has done no one any harm. I urge the citizens of Hoboken to remain calm. Do not panic!"

XXVI

CITIZENS PANIC!

Sightings Continue— Populace Freaks Out

Groups of Hoboken residents are wandering the streets, armed with sticks, baseball bats, fishnets, and three-foot-long hard salamis, looking for the white animal that has menaced the town for several nights.

Steve Nickelson, popular man-about-town and patron of the arts, leads one of these vigilante gangs. "We plan to capture the creature," Nickelson said. "We don't care how long it takes or how much salami we have to eat. We will take back our streets from this white monster."

Captain Hook's Book Nook on Newark Street reports that all copies of *Moby Dick* by Herman Melville, a story of a white whale, have been sold out. Also sold was the one copy of *I, Moby* by Winkus Winwater, the same story told from the point of view of the whale.

XXVII

BOY CLAIMS MONSTER IS PET

It's a Giant Chicken, says Arthur Bobowicz

A young resident of Hoboken claims the white monster that has been menacing the city is just a pet chicken that got lost—a very large pet chicken.

"I got her from Professor Mazzocchi," Arthur Bobowicz of 127 Hudson Street told *The Hoboken Evening News*. "He's a mad scientist who lives on Court Street."

The Hoboken City Directory does not list anyone named Mazzocchi, and the

Hoboken Yellow Pages has no entries under "Mad Scientist."

"Her name is Henrietta. She ran away, and she's probably scared," young Bobowicz said. "If you see her, be nice to her—and call me. I'll come and get her."

Other persons contacting *The Hoboken Evening News* have claimed the white apparition is the ghost of Alexander Hamilton, a Hudson River walrus, a weather balloon, and the vice president of the United States.

• XXVIII •.

IT IS A CHICKEN!

I Told You So, Says Bobowicz

Hoboken Evening News photographer Mel Snelson has gotten the first photographs of the white monster, and it is a chicken.

"It was eating some potato peelings in the alley behind the Three Star Chinese-American Lunchroom," Snelson said. "I walked right up to it and got four front views, a profile, and one of the chicken walking away. It clucked at me."

(Additional photos on Page 2.)

The mayor's office refused to confirm

or deny rumors that a professional chicken catcher, from out of town, hired by the city at considerable expense, had failed to catch the bird.

Asked for comment, young Arthur Bobowicz said, "It's a chicken. It's my chicken. It's not a monster. Her name is Henrietta. She likes potatoes. Be nice to her."

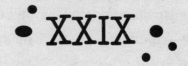

BE NICE TO THE CHICKEN

Experts Claim Kindness Is Needed

Professor Leon Watstein of Stevens Institute of Technology told *The Hoboken Evening News* that the giant chicken is probably insecure and will stop rampaging at night if treated with kindness.

Hoboken health commissioner Dr. Milton Sargon, who is also chief veterinarian for the Port of Hoboken, said, "Watstein is probably right. He studies that sort of thing."

Dr. Hsu Ting Feng, a famous Chinese poultry expert passing through town, stopped by the offices of *The Hoboken Evening News*. "Chickens are very sensitive birds. Possibly something frightened or upset this chicken, causing it to go wild. Friendly overtures and kind treatment will restore harmony."

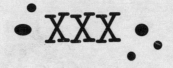

XXX

BE KIND TO CHICKEN CAMPAIGN UNDERWAY

Bird Appears Mollified

Molly Fried of the Woof 'n' Stuff pet shop told *The Hoboken Evening News*, "Several people have purchased the special Chicken Mollifying Kits we have prepared, which contain potatoes, potato chips, a chicken hand puppet, and a sheet of instructions indicating a few basic and easy-to-learn clucking sounds. Those who have met the chicken say she seems to be somewhat mollified, or soothed in temper or disposition."

XXXI

KID CATCHES BIRD

Henrietta Returns to Bobowicz

Arthur Bobowicz had just gone to bed when Henrietta appeared on the fire escape outside his window. He opened the window and let her in, hugged her, and scratched her head. Henrietta went to sleep on the rug next to Arthur's bed.

In the morning Arthur's mother, Mrs. Beatrice Bobowicz, made home-fried potatoes for Henrietta. Arthur's younger brother and sister, Henry and Lucille, played with the giant chicken. Arthur's father, Mr. Gepetto Bobowicz, telephoned

Mayor Vasolini to say that Henrietta had come home.

"The crisis is over," Mayor Vasolini is quoted as saying. "All city departments conducted themselves with professionalism, and we all learned something about being nice to chickens. I told the kid to bring the bird down to city hall to get a chicken license and have his picture taken with me, your mayor."

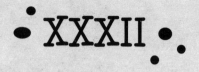

XXXII

"**S**ome story!" Bruno Ugg said.

"I want to meet this Arthur Bobowicz kid," I said. "I want to meet the chicken."

"How do you know he's a kid?" Loretta Fischetti asked. "He might be all grown up by now."

"I know he's a kid because there's his picture from the newspaper. He looks like he's about our age, maybe a year or two younger," I said.

"That newspaper could be years old," Loretta Fischetti said. "Arthur could be an adult, and the chicken could be dead. How long do chickens live, anyhow?"

Loretta had a point. Whoever had made the scrapbook had neatly cut out the articles and pictures and had trimmed off the part of each page that shows the date, and there were no dates added in pen or pencil.

"I think he's still a kid," Bruno Ugg said. "The pictures don't look like they were taken a long time ago. I mean, the people are wearing normal clothes. It looks like now."

"Easy enough to find out," Loretta Fischetti said. "People will remember something as unusual as a giant chicken rampaging through the streets. We can just ask our parents when it happened."

"While you're at it, ask them if they know where Henrietta is and if we can see her," I said.

"Yes. Let's do that," Bruno Ugg said.

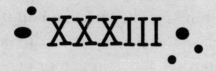

XXXIII

There ain't nobody here but us chickens
There ain't nobody here at all
So calm yourself and stop that fuss
There ain't nobody here but us
We chickens tryin' to sleep
And you butt in
And hobble hobble hobble hobble with
*   your shin*

Loretta Fischetti asked her mother if she remembered a time when a giant chicken was loose in Hoboken.

"I don't know what you're talking about," Mrs. Fischetti said.

Loretta asked her father.

"I refuse to answer," her father said. "I

didn't see anything, and I didn't hear anything."

There ain't nobody here but us chickens
There ain't nobody here at all
You're stomping around, shaking the
ground
You're kicking up an awful dust
We chickens tryin' to sleep
And you butt in
And hobble hobble hobble hobble—it's a
sin

Bruno Ugg asked his mother if she remembered anything about a giant chicken.

"I mind my own business," Mrs. Ugg said. "I know nothing. Nothing."

Bruno asked his father.

"What's a chicken?" Mr. Ugg said.

I, Nick, also known as Ivan, saw no point in asking my parents, since we'd all just moved to Hoboken. Instead, I asked Sean Vergessen, proprietor of the little corner store what he knew about Henrietta the giant chicken.

"I am D and D, kid," Sean Vergessen said. "And anything I might have known, I've already forgotten. Have a free Dr. Pedwee's Avocado-Lime Soda."

Tomorrow is a busy day
We got things to do
We got eggs to lay
We got ground to dig
And worms to scratch
It takes a lot of settin' gettin' chicks
*   to hatch*

"Well, the adults aren't talking," I said.

"We should have warned you," Bruno Ugg said. "It's a Hoboken tradition. Nobody ever gives information in response to a direct question."

"Why is that?" I asked.

"Don't ask me," Bruno Ugg said.

"I have no idea what you're talking about," Loretta Fischetti said.

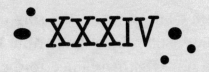

XXXIV

I was born in Hoboken
H-O-B-O-K-E-N
Where the guys are the squarest
The girls are the fairest
H-O-B-O-K-E-N

"Seriously, why won't the adults talk about the chicken?" I asked Loretta Fischetti and Bruno Ugg.

"Not sure," Bruno said. "Maybe it's because they're embarrassed."

"Embarrassed?"

"Yes," Loretta Fischetti said. "I mean, you live in a town where the local disaster wasn't a flood or an earthquake or a hurricane, but a rampage by a giant chicken. It's the sort of thing you want other people to forget about."

"I don't know—it seems sort of cool to me," I said. "I still want to find Arthur Bobowicz and find out what happened to the chicken. In fact, I want to even more now."

"So because the adults don't want to tell us, you want to find out even more?" Bruno Ugg said.

"That's right. You know, that might be a neat way for teachers to motivate kids . . . refuse to teach them."

"Oh, that's right—you haven't been to school in Hoboken yet," Loretta Fischetti said.

"They thought of it already?" I asked.

"Did they ever," Loretta Fischetti said.

"Well, I thought of something," I said. "I thought of a way to get all the info on the chicken. All we have to do is go to *The Hoboken Evening News* and look at the files. Newspapers keep records."

"Newspapers that are still in business do," Bruno Ugg said.

"It's closed down?"

"Closed and gone. It's a Barstuck's Coffee Bistro now."

"Hmmm."

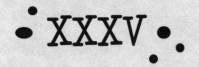

XXXV

"**W**e can ask the police. Police keep records," I said. "I have been wanting to go to the police station anyway, to report the theft of my bicycle."

"I've never been inside the police station," Bruno Ugg said.

"Neither have I," said Loretta Fischetti. "And it's just around the corner."

"Let's go," I said.

The police station was sort of underneath the city hall. We went down a couple of steps into a big room that was dark and cool. It looked just like in the movies. There was a big high desk, and there was a policeman sitting behind it. We stood in front of it, and he had to lean forward and look down to see us.

"I'm Sergeant Flooney," the policeman said. "How can the Hoboken Police Department serve and/or protect youse kids?"

"There are two things," I said. "First of all, I want to report that my bike was stolen."

Sergeant Flooney twisted around in his chair and hollered over his shoulder, "Hey, Spooney! Here's kids to report another stolen bike!" Then he turned back to us, and said, "Go over there, in a minute, and tell Officer Spooney what the bike looked like. Now what was the other thing?"

"Can you tell us anything about the giant chicken?" I asked.

"Chickens aren't a police matter," Sergeant Flooney said. "You want to see the dog warden, or maybe the pussycat warden. Now go and tell Officer Spooney all about your bicycle."

"This was a giant chicken," I said. "It rampaged through the streets."

Sergeant Flooney ran his finger down the page of a big book on his desk. "I don't see any rampages on the blotter," he said. "Like I said, chickens would be some other department. Now go see Officer Spooney. He's waiting to help you."

I told Officer Spooney about my bicycle.

"Light blue with pink hearts?" Officer Spooney asked, writing it all down. "We'll try to find it for you, but don't get your hopes up."

"Have there been a lot a bicycles stolen?" Loretta Fischetti asked Officer Spooney.

"A fair number," Officer Spooney said. "We think it's the phantom."

"The phantom?" we all asked at once.

"Did I say *phantom*? I meant to say *family*. We think it may be a family of bicycle thieves. You know, momma, poppa, kiddies— all hardened criminals. They steal 'em, paint them different colors, and sneak them onto ships—sell them in South America."

"Mine was one of those minibikes—a girl's model," I said.

"And you want it back, huh?" Officer Spooney said.

"It's the principle of the thing," I said.

"Write down your phone number," Officer Spooney said. "We'll call you if we have any news."

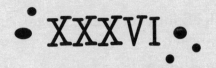

XXXVI

"**O**fficer Spooney said *phantom*," Bruno Ugg said when we were outside the police station. "Then he tried to cover it up."

"So it was the phantom who stole my bike! I suspected as much!" I said.

"And he or she has stolen other bikes too," Loretta Fischetti said.

"And the adults don't want to talk about it," I said.

"Just like the giant chicken," Bruno Ugg said.

"What is it with the adults around here?" I asked.

"I'm saying nothing," Loretta Fischetti said.

"I refuse to answer," Bruno Ugg said.

"Well, I bet I know one person who could

tell us all about everything," I said.

"Who's that?"

"Arthur Bobowicz."

"Well, he should at least be able to tell us about the chicken," Loretta Fischetti said. "But you know what?"

"What?" Bruno Ugg and I asked.

"This morning I looked up Arthur Bobowicz in the phone directory."

"And?"

"There was no Arthur Bobowicz," Loretta Fischetti said. "There was no Bobowicz, even. So you have any ideas?"

"I do have an idea, now that you mention it," I said. "Your parents and Sean Vergessen told us nothing," I said. "The newspaper is shut down. Sergeant Flooney and Officer Spooney we just met, and they were no help. But I have an idea. There is one place where you can always get information, and that place is . . ."

"Yes? That place is? Tell us!" Loretta Fischetti said.

"That place is . . . ," I said. I paused again,

just to tease the others.

"Spit it out, Nick!" Bruno Ugg shouted. "What is that place where you can always get information?"

Smiling broadly, because it was such a neat idea and I had thought of it, I said, "That place is . . . the public library!"

"Novel notion," Bruno Ugg said.

"I confess, it would not have occurred to me," Loretta Fischetti said.

"Let's go there right now," I said. "Where is it, by the way?"

"I'm pretty sure I know where it is," Loretta Fischetti said. "Let's go."

XXXVII

"**Y**es, the good old public library," I said as Loretta Fischetti led us along the broiling hot streets of Hoboken. "Repository of knowledge and learning. Treasure house of stories and poetry. The intellectual record and cultural memory of the community. Temple of wisdom." I got all this stuff off the back of my old library card from Happy Valley.

"Here we are," Loretta Fischetti said.

The Hoboken Public Library looked a little like Dracula's house in the Classics Comic. It was old-fashioned and beaten up. There were green wooden shutters over some of the windows. Some of the shutters were missing, some were broken, and some were hanging crookedly. The steps leading up to the big,

black wooden door were covered with pigeon poop. I was about to suggest that maybe the library had closed and moved away when I saw the little black wooden sign with gold letters painted on it: LIBRARY IS OPEN.

We pushed open the big black door and went inside. There was a funny musty odor, like stale cornflakes. Everything inside the library was made of marble or wood painted to look like marble. The ceiling was high, and a dim gray light came from a round skylight in the middle of it. The glass of the skylight was dirty, and there appeared to be the shadow of a dead pigeon. There didn't seem to be any people in the building.

Then we heard a voice. We knew in less than a second that it was the voice of a crazy person.

"Who enters my library?" the crazy voice called. "Stand perfectly still! I warn you that I am expert in akido, baritsu, boxing, fencing, Greco-Roman wrestling, jiujitsu, judo, karate, kendo, savate, tai chi, and yubi-waza—so you are helpless against me. Now let me see what kind of vandals and hooligans are here."

Through an open doorway, we saw some-one coming upstairs from the basement of the library. It was a woman with wild hair, wearing what looked like a gym suit with rainbow-striped leg warmers and a cape.

"Ah! It is children!" the woman said. "And fairly harmless looking. What do you wish, children? Do you know where you are? This is a li-bra-ry. Do you know what that is?"

"We know what a library is," I said. "We wish to get some information."

The crazy lady in the rainbow leg warm-ers staggered and steadied herself against a desk. "Well! That took me by surprise! Information, you say. Well, information you shall have. I am Starr Lackawanna, the official librarian, custodian, and night watchperson. How may I help you?"

"We wanted to find out about the giant chicken," I said.

"Certainly, children. Nothing easier. And there is just time to do the research. I am clos-ing the library early today. President Harry S.

Truman is going to speak down at the ferry terminal, and I am going to hear him. Now just wait there. I will be back with your giant chicken information in two shakes of a lamb's tail."

Starr Lackawanna hurried off into the dark recesses of the library.

"Am I mistaken, or is she crazy as a bat?" I asked.

"You're not mistaken," Loretta Fischetti said.

"And wasn't Harry S. Truman the president a long time ago?" Bruno Ugg asked.

"Long time ago," I said.

"But at least she didn't dummy up when we wanted to know about the giant chicken," Loretta Fischetti said.

"That's true," I said. "Finally we're making some progress."

Starr Lackawanna was back. "I found what you wanted to know," she said. "Would you care to borrow pencils to take notes? I have some scratch paper you may use."

Starr Lackawanna led us to a big table and

gave us pencils and scraps of paper. "The common name of the chicken is the Jersey Giant," she began. "It is also known as the Jersey Black Giant, but its scientific name is *Gallus domesticus*, like all chickens. It is an American chicken . . . and it is much larger than others."

This was great. Loretta Fischetti, Bruno Ugg, and I were scribbling madly as Starr Lackawanna spoke.

"The Black brothers developed the Jersey Giant here in New Jersey in the eighteen seventies. The 'black' in its name is the surname of its creators, the Black brothers. The bird comes in three varieties, black, blue, and white."

We nodded to each other. The pictures in the scrapbook had been of a white chicken.

"The Jersey Giant reaches large sizes, as its name implies. Cocks are generally thirteen pounds, hens are ten pounds, cockerels are eleven pounds, and pullets are eight pounds. They are the largest breed in the American class."

We were confused.

"Thirteen pounds? That's as big as they get?" we asked Starr Lackawanna.

"As I understand things, that is as big as any chicken in America gets," the eccentric librarian said.

"So this Jersey Giant would not stand well over six feet, would it?" we asked.

"Oh, no, children. I imagine they would be oh . . . so high." Starr Lackawanna indicated with her hand. "I hope this has been of some help, children. Now I must ask you to leave the library. We don't want to be late and miss the president's speech, do we?"

Starr Lackawanna hustled us out of the library.

"Come back again any time," she said. "Any time you want information—that's what I'm here for." She locked the big door and hurried down the street with her cape flowing out behind her and her rainbow leg warmers flashing.

"Different giant chicken," Bruno Ugg said.

"Yep, different chicken," I said.

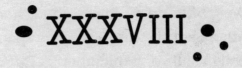

XXXVIII

Everybody's talking about chicken
Chicken's a popular bird
Anywhere you go, you're bound to find
A chicken ain't nothin' but a bird

"Dad, this is a long shot, but do you know anything about a giant chicken?"

"Do you suppose you could call me Pater? It sounds so nice. And you could call your mother Mater. It's Latin, you know."

"Never mind. I'm sorry I asked."

"Sorry? Sorry you asked about the giant chicken that terrorized Hoboken some time ago?"

"What? You know about it?" I was wild with excitement.

"Well, of course I know about it, old fig," my father said. "It was in the newspaper."

"Tell me all you remember . . . Pater," I said.

"Let me see. . . . There was this huge white creature storming about in the streets. People didn't know what to make of it—thought it was a polar bear and all sorts of things. Then it turned out to be an outlandish huge chicken. There was some more carrying on, and in the end it turned out to have been some child's pet. Ridiculous, eh? Much ado about nothing. Mind you, it was an exceptionally large chicken."

"Do you remember when all this happened?" I asked my father.

"No idea, old waffle," my father said. "Whoever had put together the scrapbook had trimmed off the part of the page that shows the date."

"The scrapbook?" I asked.

"Yes. I was rummaging in the basement a few weeks ago and found a box of old rubbish. There was a scrapbook with cuttings about the chicken. I can find it for you, if you like."

"So all you know about the chicken is what you read in that scrapbook."

"I just said," my father said. "What's the matter, old egg, you look rather disappointed."

"My friends and I found that same scrapbook," I said. "We've been trying to find out more about the chicken and the kid, Arthur Bobowicz. Also, there seems to be some sort of phantom. I think it stole my bicycle. The thing is, when we ask adults about this stuff, they don't know anything or they won't tell us what they do know. For a minute I thought you knew about the chicken and were going to tell me something."

"I see your problem," my father said. "It's deuced frustrating. You know, most adults don't feel they have time to answer the questions of you little whippersnappers. But I can tell you how to get all the local news and gossip."

"How?" I asked.

"It's simply a matter of who you ask. As I said, most adults won't give you the time of day—but here's what you must do. Look for a shabby individual, one who is a bit dirty, needs a shave, and doesn't smell very nice. This chap will often be sitting on a bench in the park. You may notice that he has a bottle of wine in a paper bag."

"A bum?" I asked.

"So to speak," my father said. "Now here's someone who has plenty of time to observe the passing parade. He's generally ignored by the rest of society—nobody wants to hear anything he may have to say. You give this fellow your respectful attention, and possibly fifty cents, and he will tell you everything he knows."

"So ask a bum in the park?"

"Do remember that some people who fit the description are psychotic and might possibly attack you. But if you're polite, keep a safe distance, and your eye on a route of escape, you should be all right. About the worst thing that may happen will be having a small wine bottle bounced off your noggin. On the positive side, you might have an interesting conversation."

"So you're recommending this?" I asked my father.

"Oh, absolutely, old nut. I talk to homeless chappies all the time myself," my father said. "Fine fellows, mostly."

On my way out the door, my mother called to me. She was on a tall ladder, chipping paint off the ceiling.

"Everything all right?" my mother asked. "Doing anything interesting?"

"I'm going to meet my friends. We're going to start conversations with alcoholic homeless men in the park," I said.

"It's another urban experience!" my mother said. "My boy is meeting life and looking it in the eye! Have a good time, Ivan!"

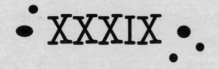

XXXIX

In the Big Rock Candy Mountain
The cops have wooden legs
The bulldogs all have rubber teeth
And the hens lay soft-boiled eggs

It didn't take us long to find Meehan the Bum. He was sitting on a bench just inside Tesev Noskecnil Park.

"He's perfect," Loretta Fischetti said. I had told her my father's requirements for a suitable bum—shabby, dirty, unshaven, bad smelling, bottle of wine in a paper bag. "Let's engage him in conversation."

"Good afternoon, sir," Bruno Ugg said. "I am Bruno Ugg, this is my friend Loretta Fischetti, and this lad we simply call Nick."

"If you're members of the Democratic Party trying to scare up votes, you're wasting your time," the bum said.

"It's nothing like that," I said. "We just wanted to wish you a good afternoon and pass the time of day."

"I am Meehan the Bum," the bum said. "I have always voted a straight Republican ticket, and the park is free to all."

"Rather than get into a discussion of politics," Loretta Fischetti said, "we wondered if you possibly recall the giant chicken that caused such a stir here in Hoboken."

Meehan the Bum took a swig from his bottle of wine and wiped his mouth with the back of his hand. He gazed over our heads, across the park, and up the Hudson River. His eyes were red-rimmed and watery.

"Giant chicken, you say? Aye, I have seen the giant chicken. I have seen the giant chicken of Sumatra, a bird too horrible to speak of. I have seen giant chickens in the hills of Kalimantan Borneo strong enough to carry away a young bullock in their beaks. See this scar?"

Meehan the Bum pointed to the knee of his greasy corduroy trousers. We nodded, although we saw no scar, only dirty fabric.

"I got this scar in a fight with a giant chicken in a back alley in Kowloon. Arr, children, I have seen more giant chickens than you have had hot breakfasts. I've seen them on land and sea, seen them in Africa and Asia and here in the States. I was chased by a giant chicken in Arizona once—had me on the run for four days. I had to climb down one side of the Grand Canyon and up the other. When a giant chicken takes a dislike to you, it's a hard bird to get away from."

"Can you tell us anything about the giant chicken that was here in Hoboken?" I asked.

"Once I was in Ulan Bator. I was having a saucer of fermented mare's milk, when this giant chicken walks up to me.

"'I suppose you think you're better than me,' the giant chicken says.

"'I think nothing of the sort,' I say. 'I am just having a quiet saucer of kumis and a poppy-seed bagel.'

"'I saw the way you looked at me when I came in,' the giant chicken says. 'You Republicans have ruined everything.'

"I can see I am going to have to fight this giant chicken. He's an ugly customer, and I wouldn't be surprised if he pulled a knife or a gun on me. So I say, 'Excuse me, but is that your order of mashed potatoes?' Giant chickens can't resist potatoes. While he is distracted, looking for the potatoes, I klonk him with a bottle and run out the door."

"How about the giant chicken right here in town?" I asked Meehan the Bum. "Have you ever run into her?"

"Well, actually, no," Meehan the Bum said. "This is the first I've heard of it."

"Oh, great," Loretta Fischetti said. "He never heard of the giant chicken. I don't suppose there's any point in asking him about the phantom."

"Why don't you ask me and see?" Meehan the Bum asked.

"All right. I'll play," I said. "Do you know

anything about the phantom?"

"Not really," Meehan the Bum said. "Except I do know where the cave is where the phantom keeps the things it steals."

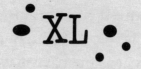

XL

"The cave?"

"Yep. Sibyl's Cave," Meehan the Bum said. "Old Hoboken Landmark. That's where the phantom keeps all the stolen goods."

"Wait a minute," Loretta Fischetti said. "I never heard of any cave in Hoboken."

"Well, there is one," Meehan the Bum said. "It used to be a popular tourist attraction. There was a natural spring in the cave, and people used to pay a penny per glass to drink the water—which was a whole lot of money for a glass of water, but they thought the water had medicinal properties. This started in eighteen thirty-two, and went on until the eighteen eighties when Hoboken got a board of health."

"Then what happened?" Bruno Ugg asked.

"Board of health closed it down. Turns out the water wasn't fit for human consumption," Meehan the Bum said.

"I've been all over Hoboken, and I have never seen any cave," Loretta Fischetti said.

"Have you ever played in the baseball field at the other end of this park?" Meehan the Bum asked.

"Yes."

"Then you were standing right on top of the cave. You know that road at the bottom of the cliff, under the baseball field, that goes alongside the river?"

"Frank Sinatra Drive?"

"Well, that's where the entrance to the cave used to be," Meehan the Bum said. "For a while there was an illegal fermented sauerkraut factory in the cave. During the nineteen thirties, this was."

"I never saw any entrance to any cave down there," Loretta Fischetti said.

"That's because they sealed it up and disguised it," Meehan the Bum said. "So kids like you wouldn't wander in and get killed."

"If it's sealed up, how does the phantom get in?" Loretta Fischetti asked. "Assuming that I believe a single word you're saying—which I do not."

"There's a secret entrance," Meehan the Bum said. "Unless you knew it was there, you'd never find it. That's how the phantom goes in and out."

"And you know where the entrance is," I said.

"That's right," Meehan the Bum said. "And I won't tell where—but I'll give you a hint: Trust Buster."

"Who's Buster?" Bruno Ugg said.

"I'm dummied up," Meehan the Bum said. "Find out for yourselves."

"We're going to check on this story, you know," Loretta Fischetti said.

"Feel free," Meehan the Bum said. "But if you ask those Democrats, they'll just lie to you. Once, in Arizona, a big Democrat chased me for four days. I had to climb down one side of the Grand Canyon and up the other.

Finally we had it out in an alley. I was afraid he would pull a knife or a gun on me...."

"He's off again," Bruno Ugg said.

"Good-bye, Mr. Meehan," I said. "Thank you for talking to us."

"Big giant chickens," Meehan the Bum said. "I've seen them on five continents. Big, mean, crazy giant chickens."

Loretta Fischetti, Bruno Ugg, and I walked quietly away and out of the park.

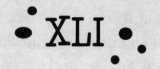

XLI

"**W**ell, he's certainly nuts," Bruno Ugg said as we walked down Washington Street.

"The stuff about the cave is interesting," Loretta Fischetti said. "I'd like to know if it really exists."

"How would we find out?" I asked.

"We could go back to the library," Bruno Ugg said.

"Starr Lackawanna?" I asked. "Would she be able to tell us?"

"She said to come back any time we wanted information," Bruno Ugg said.

"Want to go to the library now?" I asked.

"I want to get a Fudgsicle and cool out in the basement," Loretta Fischetti said. "I'm melting. Let's go see Starr Lackawanna tonight, when it's less hot."

We stopped at Sean Vergessen's store and arrived in the basement, Fudgsicles in hand, to find that someone had left part of a rusty sewing machine and half a tuna fish sandwich in the middle of the floor.

The plastic milk crate with the Classics Comics was gone.

We stood there, stunned. The Fudgsicles dripped.

"The phantom!" Bruno Ugg said. "We've been visited by the phantom!"

"Now it's personal," Loretta Fischetti said.

"It wasn't personal when my bike was stolen?" I asked.

"Now it's more personal," Loretta Fischetti said.

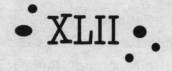

XLII

"**A**s a scientist, I do not believe in phantoms," Starr Lackawanna said.

"You're a scientist?" I asked.

"Library science," Starr Lackawanna said. "I have a master's degree. Of course, I am very sorry that your Classics Comics were taken. We don't have any comics here at the library, but we have most of the original books they're based on. You are welcome to check them out."

"*Twenty Thousand Leagues Under the Sea*?" I asked.

"Certainly," Starr Lackawanna said. "Do you all want me to issue library cards to you?"

Starr Lackawanna typed our names on three official Hoboken Public Library cards. I had her type my name as Nick Nemo. I was pretty sure she knew that wasn't really my name—but she did it anyway.

"So is Sibyl's Cave real, Ms. Lackawanna?" Loretta Fischetti asked.

"Not many people know about Sibyl's Cave," Starr Lackawanna said. "It's been sealed up since the eighteen eighties, and the entrance was covered up and concealed in nineteen thirty-seven. People were afraid that children would get lost in it."

"Like Tom Sawyer," I said. It was one of the best Classics Comics.

"Probably it was because of that book that people were concerned about children getting lost," Starr Lackawanna said. "We have that book, by the way, and I recommend it highly. But you know, there wasn't really much danger of anyone getting lost in Sibyl's Cave. It's only about thirty feet long."

"Where is the cave exactly?" Bruno Ugg asked.

"You know Tesev Noskecnil Park?" Starr Lackawanna asked.

"We were there earlier today," Loretta Fischetti said.

"The cave is said to be under the park," Starr Lackawanna said. "It's quite a nice little park, with paths and stately trees, swings and slides for little children, a baseball field, and you must have noticed the handsome statue of Theodore Roosevelt, twenty-sixth President of the United States, between nineteen-oh-one and nineteen-oh-nine, and known as the Rough Rider, the Trust Buster, TR, and Teddy. Did you know the teddy bear was named in his honor?"

"What did you say he was called? The Trust Buster?" Loretta Fischetti asked.

"Yes," Starr Lackawanna said. "He busted the trusts—meaning he was against unfair practices by big companies and groups of companies that joined together as 'trusts' to suppress competition. Did you know he also helped to negotiate the end of a war between Russia and Japan at the beginning of the twentieth century?"

"So Buster is not the name of a person,"

Loretta Fischetti said.

"Not in this connection," Starr Lackawanna said. "Theodore Roosevelt visited this very library once. We have a photograph of him being issued a library card."

We checked out *The Adventures of Tom Sawyer* by Mark Twain, *Twenty Thousand Leagues Under the Sea* by Jules Verne, and *Treasure Island* by Robert Louis Stevenson, thanked Starr Lackawanna for all the information and the library cards, and went out into the muggy Hoboken night.

"So. Trust Buster," Loretta Fischetti said.

"Meehan the Bum said it was a clue," I said. "Let's take a good look at that statue in the park tomorrow."

XLIII

I wound up taking *Treasure Island* home with me. I meant to just read the first few pages, but instead I read far into the night. When I slept, I was still with Jim Hawkins, Long John Silver, and the pirates on board the ship *Hispaniola*. When I woke up, I read some more. I had liked the Classics Comics version, but the real book was ... well ... real.

Even though I was walking and talking and being my normal self, part of me was still on the island with Jim Hawkins, Squire Trelawney, and Captain Smollett when I met with my friends. Bruno Ugg was deep into *Twenty Thousand Leagues Under the Sea*, and Loretta Fischetti was plowing through *The Adventures of Tom Sawyer*. We had agreed to inspect the Theodore Roosevelt statue in Tesev Noskecnil Park to see if we could figure out more about the "Trust Buster" clue, but under the circumstances, we decided to spend a couple of hours reading first.

Vic Trola's voice came over the radio, "That was 'I Gave You My Heart and a Diamond, and You Clubbed Me with a Spade,' by—" Someone reached out and clicked off the radio. I didn't look up to see who. We read on in silence.

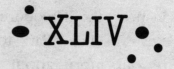

XLIV

We were in a sort of trance. Actually, three trances. When Loretta Fischetti's mother came down with turkey salad sandwiches, Cheez Doodles, and iced tea, it was as though we were suddenly awakened from sleep. We stretched and yawned and blinked. Then we realized we were wildly hungry.

The sandwiches disappeared first. The iced tea felt good going down, and the Cheez Doodles were crunchy and made our fingers and faces orangey yellow.

"What do you say, shall we go look over the Teddy Roosevelt statue now?" I asked.

"Yes, we should," Loretta Fischetti said. "If what Meehan the Bum said was true, if 'Trust Buster' is a clue to where the entrance to

Sibyl's Cave is, then we have to plan to go there and try to get back our Classics Comics."

This was the first time any of us had actually said it.

"So we are going to try to get into the cave?" Bruno Ugg asked.

"I think we have to," Loretta Fischetti said. "It has our comics."

"And some of my father's comics. He's saved them since he was a boy," I said. "I don't want to have to tell him they're gone."

"But it's the phantom's cave now," Bruno Ugg said. "And we don't know anything about the phantom, how dangerous and evil it may be."

"I think we should be careful," Loretta Fischetti said. "But I think we have to try."

"We'll just have a look," I said. "It may not be a clue at all. Most of what Meehan said sounded like raving—most likely this is too."

"Well, if we're going, let's go," Bruno Ugg said.

We emerged into the heat wave. The

citizens of Hoboken were sweating through their clothes—those who were in the street. Most people were probably indoors some-where, sitting in front of air conditioners and fans. We made our way through the town, like a bunch of exhausted reptiles.

It was a little cooler under the trees in Tesev Noskecnil Park. At moments I imagined a little breeze was starting to happen—but it never did.

There was the statue of Teddy Roosevelt, big as life, and we had never noticed it before. TR was standing on a pedestal with sloping sides. His feet were a little higher than our heads. He was staring to the south and point-ing to the southeast with his left hand. In his right hand he held a big stick.

"Wow! He looks sort of like a walrus," Bruno Ugg said.

"And look at those little goggles," I said.

"He looks determined," Loretta said.

"So where's the clue?" Bruno Ugg asked.

"This is like *Treasure Island*!" I said. "Look at his hand! He's pointing! Follow the finger!"

We crowded under the hand of the statue and tried to see where it was pointing. It was pointing to the baseball diamond.

"That's the clue? It's just ground!" Bruno Ugg said.

"What are we supposed to do, go at it with shovels?" Loretta Fischetti asked.

"I don't know. Maybe we're supposed to pry up home plate," I said.

"This is disappointing," Loretta Fischetti said.

"It's just like *Treasure Island*," I said. "Only it's a statue pointing instead of a skeleton pointing. But it's not pointing at anything in particular."

"That, or you don't know how to look," a voice said.

We turned around and saw someone sitting on a bench nearby. He had been listening to us talk. It was an old guy with long gray hair. He was wearing a Boston Red Sox jacket and silk slippers with red and gold dragons on them.

"What?" we said.

"You said the statue is not pointing at anything in particular," the old guy said. "I say you haven't explored all the possibilities."

"Such as what?" Loretta Fischetti asked the old guy.

"It's polite to introduce yourself when you converse with someone," the old guy said. "I am Sterling Mazzocchi, and to whom do I have the honor of speaking?"

We introduced ourselves. As each of us spoke our name, Sterling Mazzocchi bowed his head, and said, "Delighted."

"Such as what?" Loretta Fischetti asked again.

"Such as, has the statue always been in the place it now occupies? Has it always faced in the direction it now faces? How do you know it is pointing at the baseball diamond, when it might be pointing to something farther away?"

"But there's nothing visible beyond the baseball field but the Hudson River and New York City," I said.

"I just asked, 'how do you know?'"

Sterling Mazzocchi said. "What if you carefully lined up a powerful telescope with the pointing finger and were able to read an inscription on the building in Manhattan it's indicating? Couldn't that be the clue you're looking for?"

"Do you know what clue we're looking for?" I asked.

"You're looking for the entrance to Sibyl's Cave, carefully hidden since nineteen thirty-seven," Sterling Mazzocchi said.

"Is there an inscription on a building in Manhattan telling us where to find it?" Loretta Fischetti asked.

"There could be," Sterling Mazzocchi said. "There's no reason why there couldn't be."

"Do you know there to be such an inscription?" I asked.

"No, I do not actually know for a fact— that is, I have not seen such an inscription myself, with my own eyes," Sterling Mazzocchi said.

"Do you believe there is such an

inscription?" Bruno Ugg asked.

"No, I do not," Sterling Mazzocchi said.

"Do you know where the entrance to Sibyl's Cave is?" Loretta Fischetti asked.

"Yes. I know that," Sterling Mazzocchi said.

"Will you tell us?" I asked.

"No, I will not," Sterling Mazzocchi said.

"Why? Why will you not tell us?" Bruno asked.

"The entrance to the cave was concealed for the very reason that children might try to get into the cave, get lost, and die there," Sterling Mazzocchi said.

"But we were told the whole cave is only thirty feet long," I said.

"Yes, I believe that is so," Sterling Mazzocchi said.

"So we are not likely to be in very much danger," I said.

"Caves are dangerous," Sterling Mazzocchi said. "Anything can happen in a cave."

"Do you know about the phantom?" Loretta Fischetti asked Sterling Mazzocchi.

"Do you know what an urban legend is?"

Sterling Mazzocchi asked Loretta Fischetti.

"Yes."

"The phantom is an urban legend," Sterling Mazzocchi said.

"The phantom stole Nick's bicycle and our joint collection of Classics Comics," Loretta Fischetti said. "Can a legend do that?"

"Some legends can, apparently," Sterling Mazzocchi said.

"Do you know about the giant chicken who once menaced Hoboken?" I asked.

"Yes, I do," Sterling Mazzocchi said.

"Is that a legend too?" I asked.

"No, the chicken is quite real," Sterling Mazzocchi said.

"Do you know where it is now?" I asked.

"I have been away for a long time. You should ask someone who knows a lot about Hoboken history and lore," Sterling Mazzocchi said. "Now if you will excuse me, I have to go take my rhumba lesson." So saying, the old man got up and walked out of Tesev Noskecnil Park.

"Odd fellow," I said.

"Not as insane as Meehan the Bum," Bruno Ugg said.

"His name is vaguely familiar," Loretta Fischetti said.

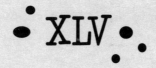

XLV

"Let's ask Starr Lackawanna if the Teddy Roosevelt statue was ever in a different location," Loretta Fischetti said. "If she doesn't know, she'll be able to look it up for us."

"When we asked her about the giant chicken, she dug up stuff about some other giant chicken that only weighs thirteen pounds," I said.

"But she's friendly and wants to help," Loretta Fischetti said. "She would have dug up more about the chicken if we had asked her—and she came through with information about the cave and accidentally explained 'Trust Buster.'"

"She gave us library cards and checked out great books to us," Bruno Ugg said. "And she is the only adult who seems to want to talk to us who isn't a crazy old man in the park."

"Okay, I agree," I said. "Starr Lackawanna is cool. Let's go talk to her."

As we came through the door of the library, Starr Lackawanna said, "Oh, children! I found more giant chicken information for you!"

Loretta Fischetti looked at us triumphantly. "What did I tell you?" she said.

"Did you know that a giant chicken, more than six feet tall, once rampaged through the streets of Hoboken?" Starr Lackawanna asked.

"Yes, we knew that," we said.

"Did you know her name was Henrietta, and she was the pet of a little boy named Arthur Bobowicz?" Starr Lackawanna asked.

"Yes, we knew that," we said.

"Did you know that the chicken went wild for a while and the citizens panicked?" Starr Lackawanna asked.

"Yes, we knew that," we said.

"And that the chicken finally calmed down and was reunited with little Arthur?" Starr Lackawanna asked.

"Yes, we knew that," we said.

"And that the chicken was bred right here in Hoboken by a mad scientist named Professor Mazzocchi?"

"We knew that, but we forgot," we said. "Did you say Mazzocchi? What was his first name?"

"Sterling," Starr Lackawanna said. "It was Sterling. I never forget a first name."

"Astonishing!" I said.

"Amazing!" Bruno Ugg said.

"Astounding!" Loretta Fischetti said.

"I live to astonish, amaze, and astound," Starr Lackawanna said. "Those are things librarians do well."

"Did you find all this out from old newspaper articles?" Loretta Fischetti asked.

"Yes, I did," Starr Lackawanna said.

"Do you know where Henrietta the giant chicken is today?" I asked Starr Lackawanna.

"No. Do you want me to keep looking up

facts?" the librarian asked.

"We are interested in Henrietta the giant chicken," Loretta Fischetti said. "But there's something we're more urgently interested in. We need to know if the Teddy Roosevelt statue in the park ever stood in a different location. Do you happen to remember?"

"I only moved to Hoboken six months ago, so I wouldn't remember personally," Starr Lackawanna said. "But we can do some checking. Come down to the basement where the maps and plans are kept."

As we followed Starr Lackawanna down the steps to the map room in the library basement, Loretta Fischetti whispered to Bruno Ugg and me, "I thought I recognized that name. The guy in the park was Professor Mazzocchi!"

"Do you think it's the same guy?" I whispered to Loretta Fischetti.

"Unless there are two people named Sterling Mazzocchi who know about the chicken," Loretta Fischetti said.

"Then it's him! We have to find him again!" I said.

"We have the phantom to deal with first," Loretta Fischetti said. "The giant chicken can wait."

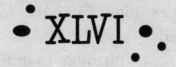

XLVI

"**H**ere's a piece of luck!" Starr Lackawanna said as she unrolled a big dusty piece of paper. "It's an aerial photograph, taken from a dirigible, probably, in nineteen thirty-nine. It shows Tesev Noskecnil Park, which was then known as Evest Linkecsno Park."

"What's a dirigible?" Bruno Ugg asked Loretta Fischetti.

"Blimp," Loretta Fischetti said.

"Hey!" Bruno Ugg said.

"Yes, it's the park all right," Starr Lackawanna said. "And here is the statue—and look! It is facing Manhattan! It was turned at some point, just as you children suspected!"

"What is that building the statue's hand is

pointing to?" I asked Starr Lackawanna.

"That would be the Hoboken Academy of Art," Starr Lackawanna said. "I read up on it. It is a fine building in the Beaux-Arts style. It was built in eighteen eighty-three and was first known as the Hoboken Academy of Beaux-Arts."

"It's an art school? Hoboken has an art school?" I asked.

"It was one. It stopped being an art school in nineteen thirty-nine. It specialized in avant-garde—that's ultramodern—art. They had classes in Impossibleism, Supersurrealism, Dynamic Double-Daddy Realism, Ishkabib-bleism, and Mama."

"Mama?"

"Like Dada, only nicer," Starr Lackawanna said. "After the art school closed, the building was used for offices, apartments, and a live poultry market. I think it's just offices now. By the way, how are you kids doing with the books you checked out? Ready for more?"

"We're going to swap around before we turn them back in," Bruno Ugg said.

"That's fine. Just remember, I have plenty of other books, and you're entitled to check them all out," Starr Lackawanna said. "Did you get what you wanted about the statue?"

"Yes, thanks," Loretta Fischetti said.

"Any time you need help, that's what I'm here for," Starr Lackawanna said.

XLVII

C—that's the way it begins.
H—I'm the second one in.
I—I am the third, and
C—I'm the fourth letter of that bird, oh,
K—I'm movin' in.
E—I'm near the n.
Oh, c-h-i-c-k-e-n,
That's the way you spell chicken

"Look! It's Vic Trola!" Bruno Ugg said.

Vic Trola was sitting at a table in the Mercury Lunchroom. He was eating a bowl of oyster stew and reading a comic book.

"Let's go in and talk to him," I said. "He knows all about Hoboken history and odd facts. We never asked him if he knew anything about Henrietta the giant chicken."

"What is it with you and that chicken?" Loretta Fischetti asked.

"I want to know, that's all," I said.

"We're supposed to be tracking down the entrance to Sibyl's Cave—and you'll remember that Vic Trola went all panicky when we asked if he knew anything about the phantom," Loretta Fischetti said. "He may be the biggest nutcase we've run into so far—and who eats oyster stew when it's one hundred degrees in the shade? In fact, who eats oyster stew at any time?"

"We'll be indirect," I said. "We'll just stop in and chat for a few minutes. Maybe he'll tell us something without meaning to."

"Say! That looks like a Classics Comic he's reading," Bruno Ugg said.

"Now I'm interested," Loretta Fischetti said. "Just act natural—like we're fans of the radio show. I'd like to know where he got that comic."

We sauntered into the Mercury Lunchroom and pretended not to notice Vic Trola at first.

"Boy, is it hot!" I said.

"I sure feel like a lemonade," Bruno Ugg said.

"Hey! It's Vic Trola!" Loretta Fischetti said. "Hi, Mr. Trola!"

"Oh, hi, kids," Vic Trola said, looking up from his disgusting oyster stew and his comic book. "You can call me Vic."

"Vic, we have certainly been enjoying the songs you play on the radio," I said.

"Yes, we certainly have," Loretta Fischetti said.

"'*C-h-i-c-k-e-n*,'" Bruno Ugg sang, "'that's the way to spell *chicken*.'"

"Don't push it," Loretta whispered to Bruno.

Vic Trola smiled a big smile. "I have old records nobody has," he said. "Come and sit with me."

We crowded into the booth.

"Yeah, I love those records you play," Bruno Ugg said. "I guess you have a big collection."

"I have thousands," Vic Trola said. "May I

buy you all a soda or a lemonade—or does anyone want a taste of my oyster stew?"

"Yich! I mean, we'll just have cold drinks, thanks," Loretta Fischetti said. "Our mothers don't want us to eat between meals."

"What comic is that?" I asked.

"It's a Classics Comic," Vic Trola said. "*Kim* by Rudyard Kipling."

"That's old, isn't it?" I asked.

"Yes, I think so," Vic Trola said.

"I don't think they sell Classics Comics anymore," I said.

"That so?" Vic Trola said. "It's a pretty good comic."

The waitress brought us glasses of lemonade.

"Thanks for the lemonades, Vic," Loretta Fischetti said.

"It's a pleasure to treat my young fans," Vic Trola said. "Not many kids like my radio station. Mostly I get older people who remember the songs."

"Well, we don't listen to any other station," I said. "So where did you get the comic?"

I could sense that Bruno Ugg and Loretta Fischetti were a little tense when I asked a direct question. I knew they were afraid that Vic Trola would freak out—but he didn't.

"My mommy," he said.

"Your mommy?"

"Yes, my mommy lives upstairs. She left it lying around. Good comic," Vic Trola said. "Usually I read action comics, like *The Silver Avenger* and *Captain Justice*. By the way, be sure to tune in tomorrow. I found some Memphis Minnie records in a garage sale— I'm going to play some of them on the air."

"So your mommy likes comics?" I asked.

"She just happened to have this one," Vic Trola said. He looked at his watch. "I have to get back to the station pretty soon. The tape I have playing will end in twelve minutes. Vic Trola slurped up the last of his nauseating oyster stew, left a tip for the waitress, and paid the tab at the cash register. "Keep listening to Radio Jolly Roger, okay?" He took a toothpick from the little toothpick dispenser, put it in his mouth, and strolled out of the

Mercury Lunchroom.

"We will!" we called after him. "Thanks again for the lemonades!"

"Well, that was normal," Bruno Ugg said.

"It was," Loretta Fischetti said. "Except that he had a Classics Comic, and ours are missing."

"It doesn't prove anything," I said. "He said he got it from his mommy. I got mine from my daddy—I mean my father. He didn't act guilty or nervous."

"Still, it's quite a coincidence, you have to admit," Loretta Fischetti said.

"The chicken song is a coincidence too," Bruno Ugg said.

"It is that," I said. "But Vic Trola doesn't seem evil or nasty or anything. He's just a harmless, music-loving, oyster stew–eating freak who lives with his mommy."

"I'd like to know where his mommy got that comic," Loretta Fischetti said. "Do you suppose it's one of ours, and someone is selling them on the streets of Hoboken?"

"I hadn't thought of that," Bruno Ugg said.

"Neither had I," I said.

XLVIII

The former Hoboken Academy of Art was across the street from Tesev Noskecnil Park.

"It's quite a fancy building," I said. "It's funny we never noticed it before."

"I guess that's the Beaux-Arts style of architecture," Bruno Ugg said. "Look at all the ornaments and doodads and wiggly things on it."

"Sort of a cross between a wedding cake and a nightmare," Loretta Fischetti said. "I like it."

"I like it too," I said. "Somebody ought to wash it."

"Let's go in and look around," Loretta Fischetti said.

We went up the wide steps and through the big front door. Inside there was an open space with a high ceiling and more Beaux-Arts stuff all over everything. There were statues built into the walls. Everything was marble, and it was as grimy and crummy as the outside. A few more steps led up to a big open lobby. There was a staircase going up, and hallways leading off to the sides. We could hear voices coming from behind closed doors, the sound of a typewriter or computer printer, and the sound of shoes walking on the marble floor—but we didn't see anyone.

"So where do you suppose the secret entrance to the cave is?" I asked.

We wandered around the lobby, looking. At the back of the lobby, underneath the staircase, was the only thing in the place that wasn't Beaux-Arts looking. It was a big metal door with flaking black paint on it. There was a paper sign glued to the door:

NO ADMITTANCE!
Sealed by order of Matthias Krumwald, Commissioner of Public Works, City of Hoboken, November 17, 1937.

"And this would be the secret entrance," Loretta Fischetti said.

"This? Some secret," I said.

"Well, nineteen thirty-seven," Loretta Fischetti said. "That's when they sealed up the cave so kids wouldn't wander in, get lost, and die."

"How do you get lost in a cave that's only thirty feet?" I asked.

"Maybe that's only the story that people believe," Bruno Ugg said. "You know, an urban myth. Maybe they sealed it up so people couldn't use the cave to make illegal fermented sauerkraut."

"Right," I said. "Meehan the Bum mentioned that. So if it's sealed, how can we get in?"

"Let's see how sealed it really is," Loretta Fischetti said.

There wasn't any handle on the door and no lock. It appeared to be attached to the marble wall with big screws. We got our fingernails around the edge and tugged. It wiggled a little. We all grabbed the edge on one side and pulled. It wiggled, but it didn't move.

Then we tried prying the other side with our fingers. The door opened a tiny bit. We got a better grip and pulled again. It swung open a few inches.

"Easy as pie," I said.

We pulled the door open enough for me to stick my head inside. I could just make out the beginning of a flight of stairs going down.

"Stairs! Carved out of the living rock," I said. "It's pretty dark, though."

"We need flashlights," Bruno Ugg said. "Shall we go get some and go exploring?"

"I think we have to," Loretta Fischetti said.

"Wait!" Bruno Ugg said. "What if the phantom is down there? What if it lives down there?"

"Good point," I said. We pushed the door closed and took a few steps back.

"You saw the phantom that time, at the Bat Hat Festival," Loretta Fischetti said. "Did it look dangerous?"

"It was tall," I said. "I just had a glimpse. I can't say whether it looked dangerous or not. I don't think I want to meet it in a cave."

"I think we should come back at night," Loretta Fischetti said.

"At night?"

"At night is when the phantom prowls the streets of Hoboken, taking people's comic books and leaving them junk and tuna fish sandwiches."

"But at night it's dark," Bruno Ugg said.

"It's a cave," Loretta Fischetti said. "It's always dark."

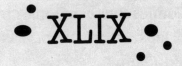

XLIX

"**W**hat's on the schedule for this evening, old graham cracker?" my father asked. He pronounced *schedule* "shed-yule."

"I'm going to explore a cave with my friends," I said. "That's why I'm borrowing the flashlight."

"Ah, the fascinating sport of spelunking, eh? Jolly good fun," my father said. "Be very careful not to fall into a pit and break all your bones, or drown in an underground pool, or get lost and starve and go mad in the darkness. Ah, youth! I wish I were going with you! But I have to stay here and strip wallpaper, dash the luck."

"Thanks for the loan of the flashlight," I told my father. I still hadn't told him that his

Classics Comics were among the missing. With good luck, I'd get them back, and he'd never have to know.

"Going out, Ivan?" my mother asked.

"Going spelunking, Mother," I said.

"Take a sweater! It gets cold in caves," my mother said.

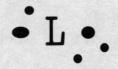

L

"**W**hat if someone locked the front door?" Bruno Ugg asked.

"I never thought of that," Loretta Fischetti said. "If we were to bust in, we'd be breaking the law."

"We're going to bust into the cave," Bruno Ugg said.

"Not really," Loretta Fischetti said. "The door to the cave isn't really locked."

"Yes, but the sign says 'No Admittance,'" Bruno Ugg said.

"'No Admittance,' in 1937," Loretta Fischetti said. "Don't official things expire after twenty-five years or something?"

"Let's just try the door," I said. We walked up the stairs and pulled the handle. The door swung open.

"Look at that. It wasn't locked," Bruno Ugg said.

"Look at that," Loretta Fischetti said.

"Yeah, look at that," I said.

We stood there in the doorway, about to enter the Hoboken Academy of Art, at night, with the intention of opening the door, officially sealed in 1937, that led to Sibyl's Cave. What if a cop came by? Would we be arrested for burglary and spelunking without a license?

A cop came by.

"Good evening, kids," the cop said. It was Officer Spooney. "Not up to any mischief, I hope."

"No, sir," we said.

"Well, don't stay out too late and worry your parents," Officer Spooney said. He continued along the street, whistling.

"Let's get inside," Loretta Fischetti said. "Everybody got your flashlight? Everybody got a hat?"

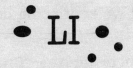

LI

The lobby of the Hoboken Academy of Art was dimly lit by a couple of dinky lightbulbs. We made our way to the metal door under the stairs, pulled it open, and pointed our flashlights down the steps. The steps went down and down. Our flashlights made three white pencils of light. They hardly made a dent in the blackness.

"Let's go," Loretta Fischetti said.

We started down. I would have thought it would be cool, like our basements, going down stairs into a cave, but the air that rose from the deep below was hot and had a sour smell.

My knees were shaking. I thought the other kids were scared, too, but no one said anything, and we kept going down, a step at a time.

"What if there are bats?" Bruno Ugg said.

"Then we'll finally get to see one," Loretta Fischetti said.

"Are you sure this is a good idea?" I asked.

"You want to go back?" Loretta Fischetti asked.

I wanted to say yes, but instead I heard myself saying, "No. Of course not."

"Right," Loretta Fischetti said. "Our Classics Comics might be down here."

"And my bicycle might be down here," I said.

"What . . . is . . . that smell?" Bruno Ugg said.

"It smells like . . . What . . . does . . . it smell like?" Loretta Fischetti said.

"It smells sort of like—," I began.

"Sauerkraut!" Bruno Ugg said. "It smells like sauerkraut!"

"Illegal fermented sauerkraut that they used to make in the cave?" I asked.

"Sauerkraut from more than sixty years

ago? And we can still smell it?" Loretta Fischetti asked.

"That's some sauerkraut," I said.

The smell was a lot stronger as we got to the bottom of the steps.

"It's the cave! We're in the cave!" Bruno Ugg said.

It was the cave all right. It looked like . . . a cave. It had a high, rounded ceiling, and everything was rough and rocky. It was mostly totally, incredibly, completely dark— blacker than the blackest night. The sauerkraut smell was intense. It was making my eyes water. It was making my head spin. The flashlight beams picked up some glints of metal and flashes of color.

"Look! Bicycles!" Loretta Fischetti said. Her voice sounded raspy. The sauerkraut fumes were making her choke.

"So it's true!" Bruno Ugg gasped. "This is where the phantom hides stuff."

"Where are the comics?" Loretta Fischetti said as she sank to the cave floor. Then she said, "The sauerkraut. I can't . . ."

My knees were giving way. I'm not sure I said the words or just thought them as I lost consciousness. "This is funny. We're being suffocated by ancient sauerkraut fumes. We kids are going to die down here, just like everyone said."

Then I thought, Uh-oh. I'm dead.

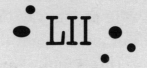

LII

So there I was, dead. Lying dead with my two friends, Loretta Fischetti and Bruno Ugg. Being dead wasn't too bad—a little boring. We just lay there. Dead. Dead as could be. Lying there. On the grass. Dead. Dead on the grass on the floor of Sibyl's Cave. Dead on the grass? On what grass? I wiggled my dead fingers and felt. It was grass, all right. There's no grass in caves. Was I in heaven already?

I had closed my eyes. It seemed like the right thing to do, being dead and all. I opened one eye and saw a white light. I had heard about this. When you die, you see a white light. Then angels come and explain to you that you're dead, and after a while God comes around and gives you a letter grade for what kind of person you had been. The lowest grade I ever got in school was B-, but it was possible that points would be deducted for going into a cave that had been sealed by the Commissioner of Public Works.

There were moths flying around the white light. I opened the other eye. It looked a lot like a streetlight, the kind they have in Tesev Noskecnil Park.

"We're in the park," Loretta Fischetti said.

"We are?" I asked.

"I think we are," Bruno Ugg said.

We sat up. We were in the park, on the grass. I could still smell the sauerkraut a little, and there was another smell—I thought it was sort of chickeny. Beside us was the plastic milk crate with our Classics Comics in it!

"Wow! I thought I was dead," I said.

"Me too," Bruno Ugg said.

"I saw you hit the floor," I told Loretta Fischetti. "Did you get Bruno and me out of the cave and rescue the comics, and if so, how did you do it?"

"I didn't do anything that I know of,"

Loretta Fischetti said. "I don't know how we got here."

"I think the giant chicken saved us," I said. I didn't know why I said that, except that was what I thought.

"Well, I can't say you're wrong," Loretta Fischetti said. "Because I don't know what actually happened, but I can say that you have that giant chicken on the brain." She brushed a white feather off her shoulder.

"It was the giant chicken," I said. "It saved us."

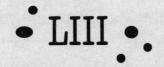

LIII

We took turns carrying the milk crate full of Classics Comics. When we got to our buildings, my father and Loretta Fischetti's father, Lance Fischetti, were sitting on the steps, smoking cigars.

"Hi, kids," Mr. Fischetti said. "How did the spelunking go?"

"We got killed," Bruno Ugg said. "But we're all right now."

"Nick thinks we were rescued by the giant chicken," Loretta Fischetti said.

"Ah, childhood!" my father said. "It's a magical fairyland of imaginary adventures."

"It's almost your bedtime, miss," Mr. Fischetti said to his daughter. "You'd better get upstairs—and you too, young Bruno Ugg."

"Be careful when you take your shower, old Fig Newton," my father told me. "Your mother and I pulled up the floor in the bathroom. Walk on the beams."

"It really was the giant chicken that saved us," I said.

"It's great, the things kids come up with," Lance Fischetti said.

"We'll see you in the morning," Loretta Fischetti and Bruno Ugg told me.

LIV

In the morning the first thing we did was check our Classics Comics. Bruno Ugg had listed them all by title and number in a notebook, and we compared the comics in the milk crate to the list. They were all there—except one.

"It seems the only comic missing is number one-forty-three," Loretta Fischetti said.

"And number one-forty-three is?" I asked.

"*Kim*, by Rudyard Kipling," Loretta Fischetti said.

"The comic Vic Trola was reading in the Mercury Lunchroom!" Bruno Ugg said.

We were silent for a while.

"Vic Trola is tall," I said.

"Vic Trola got all nervous the time we asked him if he knew anything about the phantom," Bruno Ugg said.

"Vic Trola said he got the comic from his mommy," Loretta Fischetti said.

"Which he did not," I said.

"He was reading our comic!" Bruno Ugg said.

"Which he stole from us!" Loretta Fischetti said.

"And left us a piece of broken junk and half a tuna fish sandwich!" I said.

"Which means . . ."

"Vic Trola is the phantom!" we all said at once.

"And he has my bicycle!" I said.

"He's a skunk!" Bruno Ugg said.

"Although, he probably saved our lives. It must have been Vic Trola who dragged us out of the cave when we were overcome with fermented sauerkraut fumes," Loretta Fischetti said.

"No, that was the giant chicken," I said.

"You're so sure about that. How do you

know it was the giant chicken?" Loretta Fischetti asked me.

"I just know," I said. "I don't know how I know, but I do."

"What are we going to do about Vic Trola?" Bruno Ugg asked.

"Make him give back my bicycle," I said.

"There were a number of bicycles in the cave," Loretta Fischetti said. "Officer Spooney mentioned that there had been other thefts. We should make Vic Trola give back all the bicycles."

"We're not afraid of Vic Trola, right?" Bruno Ugg asked.

"I'm certainly not afraid of him," Loretta Fischetti said. "I might give him a knuckle sandwich—except he did probably save our lives."

"I'm pretty sure that was the chicken," I said.

"We know," Loretta Fischetti said. "The point is that Vic Trola isn't scary."

"I was sort of scared of the phantom when I didn't know who it was," I said. "But

Vic Trola is more pathetic than frightening."

"That's true," Bruno Ugg said. "Being a phantom must be some kind of mental disorder. Let's threaten him first, and then suggest he seek medical help."

"We going to threaten him now?" I asked.

"There's no time like the present," Loretta Fischetti said.

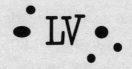

LV

"**M**aybe we should take some adult muscle with us," I said. "I mean, he is a criminal."

"The cops?" Bruno Ugg said.

"No, not the cops," Loretta Fischetti said. "They would sort of take over—and I want to confront Vic Trola myself. But I do agree, it might be a good idea to have a grown-up or two just in case he goes nuts or something."

Just then my father appeared at the head of the basement stairs. "I say, old top, are you down there? I just want your opinion—your mother and I have found this perfectly spiffing stuffed Indian fruit bat, and we wondered if you'd like it for your room." He was brandishing a very large stuffed bat with neat glass eyes. It *was* sort of spiffing, I had to admit.

"You appear at just the right moment," I told my father. "We are just going to confront the guy who stole my bicycle and were wondering if you'd like to come along and help confront."

"It sounds jolly," my father said. "You won't mind if your mother comes along too? She enjoys a confrontation as much as I do."

"That will be fine," Loretta Fischetti said.

"Topping!" my father said. "I'll just call the memsaab—and I'll bring along the fruit bat, just in case the blighter needs any persuading." He bounded off to get my mother.

"Do you understand what he says?" Bruno Ugg asked me.

"Mostly," I said.

As Loretta Fischetti, Bruno Ugg, my mother and father, and I made our way through the streets to the building where Gugliermo Marconi had once lived, I explained things to my father. "He stole our Classics Comics, but we have them all back—all but one."

"What? He took my Classics Comics as well?" my father asked. "The bounder! If he

180

offers resistance, I shall give him a bunch of fives, mark my words."

"This could never have happened in the suburbs," my mother said happily.

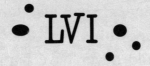

LVI

We could see Vic Trola through the picture window. He was in his living room studio, with his earphones on, broadcasting.

We all crowded in without knocking.

"Hey! It's my fans!" Vic Trola said.

"We have the goods on you, buster," Loretta Fischetti said.

"Keep your hands where we can see them, sirrah!" my father said. "This is a stuffed Indian fruit bat, and I know how to use it."

Vic Trola said things like, "Wha? Huh? Wha?"

"We know about my stolen bicycle," I said. "And the other bicycles. We know you're the phantom, and we know where you got that comic book."

"Okay, okay. I'll talk," Vic Trola said. "Just let me get off the air—and keep that fruit bat away from me."

"Make it snappy, sparky," Bruno Ugg said. "We're not playing here."

"Radio Jolly Roger now leaves the air . . . for transmitter repairs," Vic Trola said. "This is WRJR in beautiful Hoboken, New Jersey, signing off." He threw a switch and the red and green lights on the console went out. I had to admire how professional he was, even at the moment of getting busted for being the phantom.

"It wasn't me," Vic Trola said.

"Yeah, right," Loretta Fischetti said. "Who was it then, your mommy who lives upstairs?"

"I bet you don't even have a mommy living upstairs," Bruno Ugg said.

"No, my mommy lives in Florida under an assumed name. I just say it's my mommy living upstairs so people won't get curious."

"You, sir, are a rotter!" my father said. "I have a good mind to call the rozzers and have them clap the darbys on you."

"I don't know what that means," Vic Trola said. "But I ask you to allow me to tell my story."

"Very well," my father said. "But what you say had better be the emmis, or we'll give you to the peelers."

"Please be seated," Vic Trola said. "And help yourselves to dried apricots. My story is a strange and a sad one—but, speaking of strange, who is that woman tapping on the window?"

It was Starr Lackawanna. We motioned for her to come in.

"I was just out jogging, and I saw you all in here," Starr Lackawanna said. "I hope I am not interrupting."

"This man is Vic Trola. He is about to confess," I said. "These are my parents. Parents, this is Starr Lackawanna, the librarian."

"Ivan speaks highly of you," my mother said.

Starr Lackawanna flipped open a spiral notebook. "I will take down his confession,"

she said. "It's always best to make a record of such things. You may commence confessing."

"My real name," Vic Trola began, "is Arthur Bobowicz."

"Wow!" I said.

"Wow!" Bruno Ugg said.

"Wow!" Loretta Fischetti said.

"Wow!" Starr Lackawanna said, writing it down.

"Wow?" my mother and father asked.

"Years ago, when I was no older than these children, I acquired a pet from a mad scientist. It was, as most of you seem to know already, a giant chicken. I named her Henrietta. Henrietta was a good chicken, and I came to love her, but one day she ran amok."

"Amok," Starr Lackawanna said, writing it down.

"People were not used to seeing a giant chicken, six feet tall, running in the streets. I take it you all know the story of the general panic that ensued."

We nodded. We all knew.

"Once things had calmed down and

Henrietta had come home, my life was normal. I was just an ordinary boy, with a pet giant chicken. I grew up. I attended the Columbia School of Pirate Broadcasting. In time, I realized my life's dream and opened a pirate radio station, right here in this house, once the residence of Gugliermo Marconi.

"My chicken remained with me through the years. Often in the evening, we would take walks in the park and swing on the swings and slide on the slides in the children's playground, as we had done since I was a child. I was happy in my work, broadcasting songs to the citizens of Hoboken."

"I like to swing on swings and slide on slides," Starr Lackawanna said. "Did you ever go on dates?"

"It's difficult to find women who want to go on dates that include a giant chicken," Vic Trola/Arthur Bobowicz said.

Starr Lackawanna made a note in the margin. "Continue," she said.

"My life was simple but satisfying. And then I became aware that Henrietta was going out by herself at night. At first I thought nothing of it. Then I discovered that she was making tuna fish sandwiches. I could tell because she is rather messy in the kitchen, being a chicken. It seemed strange because she herself hates tuna fish. Why was she making the sandwiches, and what was she doing with them?

"Like so many others, I heard stories of a phantom, a mysterious creature that took things, and left broken machinery . . . and tuna fish sandwiches in their place. I didn't make a connection at first. Then I began to suspect—but I refused to believe it could be *my* chicken. I knew she was a good chicken—she could never take bicycles that did not belong to her—it had to be a strange coincidence.

"But then she began to bring things home, especially the bells off bicycles. I would hear her ringing them in the night. On some level I knew she was the phantom, but still I refused to admit it to myself. I remembered the public outrage when she had run amok—

but then she didn't actually do anything wrong; she just rampaged a bit. I didn't want to think of the consequences if she were stealing things.

"When you children came here and asked me what I knew about the phantom, I panicked. I knew events were closing in, and soon she would be discovered. I knew I would have to do something. I had almost made up my mind to go to the police—and then you all came here and confronted."

"Where is the chicken now?" I asked.

"She is upstairs, in her room," Arthur Bobowicz said. "I heard her ringing a bicycle bell a little while ago."

"Could you go and get her?" I asked.

"Certainly," Arthur Bobowicz said. "I will bring her right down—but first, I would like to say, I am glad you confronted. I feel sad, but strangely relieved."

Arthur Bobowicz left the living-room studio.

"I don't think he is a bad man," Starr Lackawanna said. "Just profoundly odd."

"Growing up with a giant chicken as a pet might do that to a person," my mother said.

"He is more to be pitied than censured," my father said.

LVII

Arthur Bobowicz returned with Henrietta. She was wonderful. I had never seen a chicken I liked so much, let alone one that was six feet tall. There was something tender and sad in her beautiful red eyes. I felt a great warmth coming from her.

"Ohhh, she's lovely," my mother said.

"Gee," Bruno Ugg said.

"Gosh," Loretta Fischetti said.

"Who's a pretty bird?" my father said.

"CLUCK!" Henrietta said.

"We all admire Henrietta," Starr Lackawanna said.

"She is a good bird," Arthur Bobowicz said. "But why has she turned into a phantom, and why is she doing bad things?"

"I believe I can answer that," a voice said. Someone else was in the room.

We turned and saw a man with long gray hair, wearing a Boston Red Sox jacket and silk slippers with red and gold dragons on them.

"Professor Mazzocchi!" Arthur Bobowicz said.

"Yes, Arthur, it is I. I am happy to see you all grown up into a profoundly odd adult. And what a fine bird Number Seventy-three has become! She is one of my finest superchickens, and I am proud of her."

"She's gone bad, Professor," Arthur Bobowicz said. "She's become a phantom, and she steals things."

"Yes, yes, I know all about it. That is the reason I have come back to Hoboken. I am here to help you. And Henrietta does not realize she is stealing. She is merely exchanging. She means no harm."

By this time I was standing right next to Henrietta. I hugged her. "I am sure she means no harm," I said.

"You know all about it?" Arthur Bobowicz asked.

"Indeed I do," Sterling Mazzocchi said. "When one is a mad scientist, so many of one's experiments go wrong, turn out evil, try to destroy the planet—it happens again and again. One learns to deal with it."

"How does one deal with it?" I asked.

"Well, usually I leave town," Sterling Mazzocchi said. "But I like to help when I can."

"And in this case?" Arthur Bobowicz asked.

"I can," Sterling Mazzocchi said. "An experimental giant chicken is sort of a blank slate. You don't know what to expect because it's never existed before. I bred my superchickens not only for size but for personality and sweetness of temperament. And, as you can see, Henrietta is a charming sort of chicken."

"She certainly is," I said, stroking her soft feathers.

"But, I have noticed," Sterling Mazzocchi continued, "that about twenty years on, my chickens tend to exhibit some little oddities. Phantomic behavior is common. So I came to Hoboken, to see how Number Seventy-three was getting along and to offer some help if I could."

"Deuced marvelous. The man's a wonder!" my father said.

"So you can help her?" Arthur Bobowicz asked.

"It's not as simple as just giving her an injection of Mazzocchi's all-purpose curative Number Fourteen, or fitting her with a Mazzocchi Thought-Correcting Helmet," the professor said. "I tried those things on some of the others. What will help Henrietta is a change in the way she's treated."

"What do I have to do?" Arthur Bobowicz asked.

"Well, you see, Arthur, it's not something you, personally, can do. Henrietta is your chicken, and she loves you, but . . . well, you are all grown up and busy with your fine pirate radio station and . . . well, to put it as delicately as I can, you can't communicate with her the way you did when you were a boy."

"I can't?" Arthur Bobowicz asked.

"Oh, it's not that you have neglected her, and even if you were to spend a great deal more time with her, she might still do wild things. It's like this—in some Asian countries water buffalo are used in much the way we would use a tractor. Those beasts are no different from the wild version of the same animal—an ugly customer, bad tempered, strong, and unpredictable. Do you know how they tame them, and who looks after them? Boys! Little boys! They send out these little fellows on the backs of great big buffalo with huge horns, and the buffalo are as docile as moo-cows. It's often been observed that children and youngsters can control horses no adult can come near.

"Just look at Henrietta now, and your young friend . . . what is the name? Nick? See how calm and affectionate she is? She's content. She trusts him, and he trusts her. She won't be going out to trade tuna fish sandwiches for bicycles this night, I promise you."

"So what you're saying we have to do is?" Arthur Bobowicz asked.

"I am saying, Nick here is a fine boy. Nick, you are a boy who trusts a chicken, and I like that. Would you be willing to spend some

time with this chicken every day or so? Take her around with you, play with her, just allow her to keep you company while you study or read?"

"Sure," I said. "There is nothing I'd like better."

"Henrietta is welcome at the Hoboken Public Library," Starr Lackawanna said.

"And Henrietta can hang out in our basement where we like to read, and listen to Vic Trola . . . uh, Arthur Bobowicz, on the radio," Loretta Fischetti said.

"Well, if that is so, then the chicken will soon be rehabilitated," Sterling Mazzocchi said. "All it takes is a bit of kindness."

"Oh, this is such an urban thing to have happen!" my mother said. "A giant chicken! This is the kind of rich life experience your father and I wanted you to have."

My father patted me on the shoulder. "Jolly good show, old man," he said.

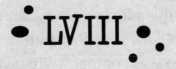

LVIII

"**A**ll that remains is to get those bicycles out of the cave," I said.

"Only there are lethal fermented sauer-kraut fumes down there," Loretta Fischetti said. "Which apparently have no effect on giant chickens—yes, Nick, I agree it was Henrietta who saved us—but humans can't go down there."

"I can help you," Professor Mazzocchi said. "I happen to have my Mazzocchi Feather-Weight Diving Helmet in my station wagon. I will be happy to bring the bicycles out."

We trooped across Tesev Noskecnil Park, Professor Mazzocchi carrying his diving helmet. Then eight of us, seven humans and the chicken, stood around in the lobby of the

Hoboken Academy of Art while Sterling Mazzocchi handed up the bicycles, one by one. Mine was there, and nine others, all shapes and sizes. We wheeled them through the lobby and lined them up on the sidewalk.

"What now?" I asked. "Do we call the police?"

"No, let's take a ride," my father said. "Three times around the park and then we'll deliver them to the constabulary in person. Everyone agree?"

"There are nine of us, including Henrietta," Starr Lackawanna said. "Can the chicken ride a bike?"

"She stole them. What do you think?" Arthur Bobowicz asked.

"Oh, Arthur, you're so droll," Starr Lackawanna said. "But we're still a rider short."

"I think I see Meehan the Bum," I said. "Hey, Mr. Meehan, can you ride a bike?"

"I finished fourth in the Tour de France," Meehan shouted back.

So we all mounted our bikes. We must have made a strange picture, kids, normal grown-ups, the not-so-normal Meehan and Professor Mazzocchi, on bikes of all sizes, and a giant chicken riding one of those adult tricycles. We pedaled slowly, making a big, graceful circle around the park, laughing and talking. Then we made another. As we began the third time around, the leaves began to tremble above us, and a cool breeze blew in from New York Harbor.

Turn the page to see what's next in store
for Nick Itch, Loretta Fischetti, Bruno Ugg,
and Henrietta, the 266-pound chicken, in

The Artsy
Smartsy Club

I

There's a point in the summer when things slow down. It's after the Hoboken Bat Hat Festival and the Fourth of July, and before Old Hoboken Days and the Italian street fair that comes just before school begins. The whole town seems to go slower, one day runs into the next, lots of people go away on vacation, and the streets are kind of empty. It feels like summer is going to go on forever, and my friends Loretta Fischetti and Bruno Ugg and I were caught in the middle of the slowness.

The library was closed. Our friend Starr Lackawanna, the librarian, was away on a kayaking holiday in Baffin Bay. Vic Trola, the pirate disc jockey, was visiting his mother in

Henfanger, Florida, and Radio Jolly Roger, the pirate radio station, was off the air while Vic Trola was away. This made the whole town seem strangely quiet. Everybody in Hoboken listens to that station.

My parents were busy prying up old linoleum, scraping woodwork, and trying to restore our 120-year-old house, something they'd probably be doing for the next twenty years. We weren't going to be taking a vacation or going on any weekend jaunts. Loretta Fischetti's and Bruno Ugg's families were busy working, and not planning any trips either. We were stuck in the city—all of us kids—with nothing in particular to do. We kicked around the streets. We read books in the basement of Loretta and Bruno's building. We took Henrietta to Tesev Noskecnil Park and played on the slide and the swings.

Henrietta is my giant chicken . . . six feet tall and 266 pounds. Henrietta isn't exactly my chicken. For a long time, she belonged to Arthur Bobowicz, better known as Vic Trola, his disc jockey name. Vic had her since he was a kid my age. But he got to be very busy running his pirate radio station and wasn't paying enough attention to Henrietta. This led to Henrietta going off by herself and getting into trouble.

Professor Mazzocchi, the mad scientist who had created Henrietta in the first place, suggested that Vic Trola sort of lend her to me—more or less permanently—I guess because he noticed how much Henrietta and I liked each other. It's just the same as though she were really my chicken. I wouldn't have it any other way.

We were on our own—three kids and a giant chicken. We did a fair amount of exploring. We hiked along the streets, visiting every block and every alley in town. We watched the trains and saw tugboats come in and out at the dock next to the railroad station. We spat in the Hudson River. We were starting to get bored. We really really needed to find something, something interesting.

II

We were wandering around down by the railroad station, feeding marshmallows to Henrietta. Henrietta loves marshmallows, and she has a special way of eating them— we toss a marshmallow up over her head, and she catches it on the tip of her beak, then she bounces it—once, twice, three times—before gobbling it down. The plan is to teach her to juggle three marshmallows, but we haven't worked out exactly how to do it.

"The problem is, she keeps eating them," Loretta Fischetti said.

"Maybe we could switch to something she can't eat," Bruno Ugg said. "Like golf balls."

"Only then she might get confused and swallow a golf ball," I said.

"True," Bruno Ugg said. "That couldn't be good for her."

We were walking along as we talked, tossing marshmallows to Henrietta. Just as we got to the statue of Sam Sloan, Loretta Fischetti saw something amazing.

"Look at that!" Loretta Fischetti said, pointing down at the pavement.

Someone had drawn a picture with colored chalks. It was more than a picture—it was like a painting. The colors were sort of magical, and it didn't seem flat—you could look deep into it. Around the picture there was a fancy gold frame, done in chalk, with loops and curls. A real artist had done it, that was obvious.

But what was really amazing was the subject of the picture. It was a big white chicken, bouncing a marshmallow on its beak! It was Henrietta!

"How do you suppose that got there?" I asked.

"Obviously someone drew it," Loretta Fischetti said.

"It must have been some fast drawer," Bruno Ugg said.

"You think that someone saw us and drew this picture just now, while we were over there by the station?" Loretta Fischetti asked.

"What else is there to think?" Bruno Ugg asked. "Whoever did this got the marshmallow and everything. I wonder where they went."

"I don't think you can draw a picture like this in a couple of minutes," I said.

"Look, we are always around with Henrietta, and we toss marshmallows to her all the time," Loretta Fischetti said. "Obviously the person who drew the picture has seen us and did the picture, but not before yesterday."

"You mean did it from memory?" Bruno Ugg asked. "That impresses me even more."

"Why not before yesterday?" I asked Loretta Fischetti.

"Because it rained yesterday," Loretta Fischetti said. "The rain would have washed away the chalk."

"It's a really good picture," Bruno Ugg said. "I wish we could take it with us."

"So do I," Loretta Fischetti said.

"It's a really good picture," I said.

III

Loretta Fischetti and Bruno Ugg live in the apartment building next door to my house. Their basement is sort of our clubhouse. We usually wander in, one by one, sometime after breakfast. We might read, or talk, or listen to cowboy songs and blues on the old radio— when Vic Trola is in town and Radio Jolly Roger is on the air. When we go out to do things, Loretta Fischetti and Bruno Ugg's basement is where we start, and when we come back, that's where we wind up.

The morning after the day we found the chalk drawing of Henrietta, I was the first one to arrive. I had grabbed an oatmeal cookie, a slice of cold pizza, and a glass of milk; given Henrietta her morning chicken kibble; and headed for the basement next door while my parents were still brushing their teeth. I figured it would be at least an hour before Loretta Fischetti and Bruno Ugg showed up, and there was something I wanted to do.

I had dug out my old Junior Artist sketchbook and a box of thirty-two crayons, most of them with the points still pointy. I settled down on the old couch—Henrietta curled up at the other end. I flipped open the sketchbook and got to work.

It was a picture of Henrietta. I was trying to do it like the chalk drawing we had seen, with red drapes behind and to one side of Henrietta, and clouds in a blue sky in the distance. The time flashed by. . . . I must have been drawing for an hour, and it seemed like a minute, when I heard someone coming down the stairs. Henrietta gave a cluck that was in between "Hello" and "Warning! There's someone coming." Henrietta is a great watchchicken.

I slid the sketchbook under the couch and stuffed the crayons into their box, which I slid behind a cushion. I wasn't sure why I didn't want the other kids to see what I was doing, but I didn't. Probably I was afraid they would think I was silly.

I didn't have to worry. Loretta Fischetti was clunking down the stairs with a whole easel—the kind they have in kindergarten, with five jars of poster paint arranged in little holes along the bottom.

"Where'd you get that?" I asked Loretta Fischetti.

"Saved it from when I was little," she said. "I'm going to do some painting."

"I brought crayons and a sketchbook," I said, bringing them out.

"Cool," Loretta Fischetti said. After giving Henrietta a good-morning head scratch, she unfolded her easel. She had to sit on a milk crate to be at the right height to paint on it, because it was little-kid-sized. Loretta Fischetti started in on her own version of the Henrietta picture.

Bruno Ugg turned up. "What's this? Baby art class?" he asked.

"Was Rembrandt a baby?" Loretta Fischetti asked. "Was Picasso a baby? Was ... what's the name of another famous artist?"

I couldn't think of one.

"Beethoven?" Bruno Ugg suggested.

"He did music, not art," Loretta Fischetti said.

"Anyway, I only meant that you are using baby art supplies," Bruno Ugg said. "Whereas, I have"—he produced a slim metal box from his pocket—"genuine professional water-colors."

"Oh, yes, I see you have the Happy Kitten brand, favored by great painters of the past," Loretta Fischetti said.

"I need a sheet of paper," Bruno Ugg said.

I tore a page from my Junior Artist sketch-book.

"Here," I said. "Knock yourself out."

IV

We labored away at our pictures. There was no sound in the basement but our breathing and Henrietta's quiet snoring. Time passed.

"Mine's finished," Bruno Ugg said.

"Mine too," Loretta Fischetti said.

"I've gone about as far as I can go with this one," I said.

We taped our pictures to the wall and looked at them.

"They're good," Bruno Ugg said.

"In a crummy way," I said.

"But they're not like the picture on the pavement," Loretta Fischetti said.

"No," Bruno Ugg said. "Nowhere near."

"Let's go and look at that picture again," I said.

At the words "Let's go," Henrietta woke up and was on her feet.

"Good idea," Loretta Fischetti said. "Let's go."

Henrietta headed for the stairs, and we hurried after her.